THE RUSTLE ... ACROSS A ... THE CREAK (... ING HOUSE .

Tamson Rawlins was abruptly awakened. She listened to the sounds emanating from her dressing room. Defiantly, she determined to face the maker of those ominous noises once and for all, she would unveil the dreadful secret of Harlequin House and find out who haunted her nights; an evil prankster or a legendary ghost.

Frightened and lonely in her husband's ancestral plantation, Tamson ran to glimpse the night's intruder. As she touched the now-empty dressing room wall, her hand came up wet—with blood!

She shuddered with the certain knowledge that the blood was a warning to her—to leave Harlequin House and the strange, brooding husband she had come to love. . . .

ELIZABETH
TEBBETTS TAYLOR

HARLEQUIN HOUSE

LEISURE BOOKS ❧ NEW YORK CITY

A LEISURE BOOK

Published by

Dorchester Publishing Co., Inc.
6 East 39th Street
New York, NY 10016

Printed in the United States of America

1

My life had been a very placid and sheltered one up to the day of my marriage—perhaps too much so, for I was ill prepared for the drastic alteration of my existence that was to follow, or the unknown terrors that would come to fill my days.

Fortunately, I had no girlish illusions about my marriage itself. I knew that for both of us it was, and would remain, one of convenience only. We both preferred it that way.

Everyone I knew in Boston that spring of 1869 thought that my marriage to Breckenridge Rawlins was both brilliant and suitable. The war had been over long enough for a southerner of aristocratic background to be civilly received in the best drawing rooms on Beacon Street.

Only Mr. Rawlins and myself knew the truth, that the marriage on his part had been one solely of financial gain, and on my part one of escape from misery and humiliation. And there was one thing I could be thankful for; I had no living relatives, and few close friends, who might read between the lines and discover the truth.

Judge John Campbell, who had been my legal guardian up to this time, knew little of my personal affairs. Up to the time of my wedding, which was held in the Campbells' home in Boston, I had seen little of them. In the six years following the deaths of my parents in a cholera epidemic, I had been at Hollowell Academy, a boarding school for young ladies in upper New York.

The war years were rather dull ones for me, and I did not leave Hollowell until the spring of 1867, when I graduated. One of my classmates, Lucy Napier, was being given a graduation ball at her aunt's estate, and we were all invited. I had always felt closer to Lucy than to my other friends, for though she had no wealth of her own, she was an orphan, as I was.

It was natural, I suppose, that there were a great many young military men present at the party, happy now that the war was over, happy to forget about duty and past hardships in a round of gaiety. I remember that Lucy's aunt's home was lavish, set amongst great gardens, and it was in the rose garden next to the house that I first saw John Markham—Captain Markham, late of General Sherman's army.

I was standing in the shadow of a small

summerhouse, and he was bending over a stone sundial trying to make out the time, with his own gold watch in one hand. He was trim and handsome in his blue uniform, with his light hair burnished bronze by the setting sun.

My skirt must have rustled or I inadvertently made some slight sound, for he glanced up suddenly, his keenly chiseled face instantly alert. When he saw me he smiled, his lips wide and boyish, and snapped his watch-case shut and slipped it into his pocket in one swift motion.

"Well, I seem to have been wasting my attention checking the time, instead of looking for a more worthy attraction. I'm John Markham. You must be one of Lucy's lovely companions?"

I smiled in return and walked out to meet him, liking the way his blue eyes widened and brightened with interest.

"Yes, Lucy and I attended Hollowell Academy together. I'm Tamson Yorke."

He screwed up his very blue eyes. "Not related to the ship-owning Yorkes—old Commodore Wylie Yorke, of Salem?"

I laughed. "Yes. He was my grandfather."

"Good lord, you're an heiress!"

I sobered at once, for I didn't like being reminded of it, mainly because Judge Campbell had warned me about fortune-seeking males.

But Captain Markham was plainly amused by the whole idea. I supposed that after living through the horrors of war, such things didn't have the same value for him as they might for other men. He was vital and handsome, and possessed of an electric something that drew me to him instantly. He reached out to take my hand and boldly tucked it under his elbow. Near to him, I could smell the odors of tobacco and some intensely masculine pomade on his crisp light hair.

"Come," he said, "I have things to show you."

His words had been only too prophetic. He had danced nearly every dance with me that night, and had taken me in to supper. The following afternoon he called to take Lucy and me driving, behind his handsome bay team. After that, my lonely, sheltered life was miraculously changed. It was wonderful to attend the theater, the art galleries, the fashionable teas, the trotting parks, with so lively and gallant an escort.

I knew I was falling in love with him; it seemed inevitable. He was handsome, charming, and devoted, and I needed no one else.

Then one balmy summer day John took me sailing at the seashore. Lucy had been unable to go with us at the last moment, due to a slight fever, but both she and her aunt had insisted that John and I go anyway. I think it was the happiest day we spent together. The sun was bright but not too hot, the sea and sky a clear faultless blue, and the breeze that ruffled our hair was like a light caress. Later, we dined at one of the old waterfront inns.

The Bowsprit, John told me, had been well known even in Washington's day, and I found it very quaint, with a huge stone fireplace and great high-backed booths that shut each table in by itself, almost like private little dining rooms. We ate cod chowder, and lobsters, and ended the meal with a rich Indian pudding. John had had wine with his meal, though I had accepted none, and he was just finishing the brandy he had ordered with our coffee, when a voice said loudly from the booth next to ours:

"Is that you, Markham?"

Across from me I could see John stiffen.

A man came around the partition. A tall, broad shouldered, muscular figure, with a dark, sardonic, bitter face under a wide brimmed Panama hat. He swept off the hat at sight of me with a lean hand, but there was insolence rather than appreciation in his gaze. And because his glance towards John was so vitriolic, I disliked him on the spot.

John seemed to awaken from the trance he had gone into at the sound of the stranger's voice, and put out his hand slowly, saying, "Hello, Rawlins, how are you? The war's over, for both of us. May I present Miss Tamson Yorke—Captain Breckenridge Rawlins, late of the Confederate Army. We graduated from West Point together."

To my embarrassment, for it had never happened to me before, he took my hand in an iron grip and kissed it. His lips seemed to sear my skin like a burning brand. His dark eyes met mine for an instant before I lowered my lashes, and I could see that he was slightly older than John, an intense, angry man with a temper that was only lightly held in check. I felt that under certain circumstances he could be a very dangerous man. But he left a moment later, and I completely dismissed him from my mind.

It was on the way home that John proposed, and I said yes at once. I had never known such happiness. John was all I had ever wanted.

I had moved in temporarily with the Campbells, and in the weeks that followed our engagement, we were kept busy attending the dinners and receptions that were given for us. I was so happy and so rushed, that at first I did not notice the change in John. He seemed to drink more than was good for him, and several times he was late coming for me, though we were usually among the first to leave a gathering. He did all the things a fiance is expected to do, sent me flowers and candy, and sometimes books of poetry, but it was all done more as a ritual he was performing than a gay impulsiveness of a man in love.

Then, suddenly, everything came to a head at the ball Lucy Napier's aunt gave in our honor. I remember it as a beautiful summer night, with all the windows and French doors of the ballroom open to the faint breeze. John and I had just finished a waltz, when he asked to be excused for a moment.

"I'll fetch you some punch," he said,

patting my arm with his white gloved hand. I smiled at him and nodded. I was standing by open French doors, and I wandered out on the stone terrace. Below me lay the rose garden, with the glow from a half moon outlining the sundial where I had first seen John. The air was scented with the odor of flowers and I wandered down the steps towards the summerhouse a few paces away. I didn't go in however, but turned in the other direction that led to the formal front gardens edged with high boxwood hedges. It was quiet here with only the sounds of birds rustling in the leaves, and the faint sound of music coming from the house. I didn't stay long, for I knew John would be looking for me. I increased my pace and swept by the summerhouse, then I stopped suddenly in my tracks. By the sundial, a man and a woman were locked in each other's arms. The moonlight glinted on uniform buttons and epaulettes, and burnished the top of the man's light hair that I knew was like no other. My hand went to my mouth as I heard him whisper:

"Lucy, my little Lucy! I've been mad these past few weeks, absolutely mad!"

"Hush," she said, putting her fingers on his lips, "you did what you had to do. I understand."

"No," he said, "no—"

And then I could stand it no longer and walked straight towards them, my head up and my eyes bright with the tears I was determined not to shed in their presence.

They both glanced up like guilty children as I approached. Lucy cried out softly, but John was silent.

"I think," I said, hoping that my voice did not sound as strained and shaken to them as it did to me, "that I am entitled to an explanation."

John stepped away from Lucy. "Tamson, you must forgive me. This is not Lucy's fault, it's mine. And it is not what it looks like— nothing has been going on behind your back. I tried—I thought—I loved you. But I have orders to go West, and I find I cannot go— without Lucy." He bowed his head and his bright hair and chiseled face had never seemed more attractive. My heart shriveled up inside me like a cinder that would disintegrate at a touch. I wanted to cry out, to beat on his chest with both my fists, and then I heard him say:

"Look, Tamson, I never meant to hurt you. But all that money—you've got to be careful. People—men, will be after your money."

A roaring anger filled my head. "You're a fine one to tell me that!" I cried.

"I know," there was genuine regret in his voice, "but it wasn't just your money. I really thought that you and I could be content together."

"Content! Is that what you think a wife wants?"

"Forgive me—us?" Lucy whispered. She was crying, but my own eyes were dry, my face solid as stone. I was numb with shock, sick with anger and humiliation, but my Puritan pride forced my lips to form the words.

"Go—please go. I never want to see either of you again."

Then they were gone. I was alone in the rose garden with the half moon still shining above, the heavy scent of roses filling my nostrils, and only a cold deadness in my heart.

I wanted to flee, but I knew I couldn't walk through the house at this moment. I needed a respite, a minute to gather my thoughts. I turned back towards the summerhouse and ran blindly into its protecting darkness. I kept on across the floor boards towards the rear where I remembered seeing a bench. As I moved, heedless of my hate of the darkness, my foot stumbled over something, and a hand reached out of the blackness and grabbed my arm.

In a panic, I cried out—just as a match flared in front of my startled eyes. The sudden light blinded me, but I could smell the strong fumes of whiskey, and feel the hot fumbling of male hands.

And then I fainted.

2

I awoke to movement, and to the feel of someone gently chafing my wrists. My head was resting against something yielding that smelled faintly of spirits. Whiskey. Suddenly I sat up alarmed. The man sitting next to me, against whose shoulder I had been leaning, laughed faintly and said, "Glad to see you've recovered, Miss Yorke."

We were riding slowly in a buggy, but I could see that we were not alone; there was a liveried driver up front. The sight of him brought me courage. I turned once more to the man who had spoken. His face was in shadow, but as we neared a cleared space in the road the moon shone down on us brightly.

I gasped, and the man inclined his dark head slightly at my sign of recognition.

"I see you remember our brief meeting, Miss Yorke?"

"Captain Rawlins!"

"I make a specialty of rescuing damsels in distress, especially if John Markham is involved." A note of grimness had crept into his tone.

"You listened," I accused hotly, "you heard everything we said!"

"Every word."

My chin came up. "You should have made yourself known, sir. No gentleman would think of—"

He broke in, "Let's get one thing straight, Miss Yorke. I am no gentleman. My manners, and my training, in most instances, do not fall too short of the mark, but I reserve the right to make use of my—shall we call them, eccentricities? I had no intention of adding to your troubles by my unwelcome presence." Then under his breath I heard him mutter, "Markham is a fool."

"Where are we going?" I asked, somewhat subdued. I disliked him, but I realized that he had gotten me out of a trying situation.

"Jason and I are driving you home," he said.

"You know where I live?"

He seemed amused. "I know a great deal about you, Miss Yorke. As a matter of fact, I would like to call upon you tomorrow, when you are more—rested."

I said nothing. I had no wish to have him call upon me. I did not like or trust him, but at least his presence was keeping me from giving way to my sorrow. I would do that, I knew now, only in the privacy of my own bedroom.

We did not speak again until we reached the Campbell house, and he handed me down from the carriage. At the door he stood apart from me, a looming shadow, and asked, "May I call tomorrow?"

"I really don't—"

"Please," he said quickly before I could refuse outright, "it could be important to you. I think you'll *want* to see me, as a matter of fact." Again there was that slightly amused tone in his voice.

I was tired and I only wanted to get away from him, from everyone. "All right," I said, and then as an afterthought added, "thank you."

In my bedroom, I flung myself across the counterpane and wept wildly into my pillow until my eyes were red and my face swollen almost beyond recognition. My world had crumbled and I didn't know which way to turn. I had built my whole future, all my dreams, on John and our marriage. I knew that people would talk, and that it would be worse for me, being a very rich girl, but that was a small thing compared to losing John. Why had he asked me to marry him, I thought wildly, why? Was it my money? Or did he honestly think, at first, that we could be happy? But he had used the word 'content'—no man asking a woman to marry him would use that word in connection with a real marriage. My head spun and my senses reeled with the agony of my thoughts, and then in sheer misery and exhaustion, I fell into a deep and troubled sleep.

I awoke early, before the household had roused, still wearing the gown I had worn to the ball. I got up wearily, the hopelessness of my thoughts already upon me, and changed into a gown and robe. I washed my ravaged face, and sat down before the dressing table to do what I could to repair my looks. I took down my thick brown hair and did it again in a more sedate manner, suitable for daytime, but I cared little how I looked. There was a picture of John on the dresser and I turned it face down. A bitterness rose up in me that I had never known before.

Someone tapped at the door, and at my bidding a maid entered. She carried morning tea on a tray and looked rather flustered.

"I heard you up, Miss, and brought your tea."

"Thank you, Nan, but I don't want any this morning. And I would appreciate it if you would help me pack later on."

"Yes, Miss Yorke. But Judge Campbell would like a word with you, as soon as you come downstairs."

I was surprised. I knew the Judge left very early in the mornings, an old habit of his, and he would never think of asking to see me at such an hour, especially since he knew that I had attended a ball the night before. It could only be something important.

"I'll dress and be down at once."

"Very well, Miss."

I dressed quickly, heartsick now that perhaps word of John and me had reached him. I did not feel capable of discussing the matter with anyone as yet. I went out into the hall, and down the curving staircase with feet like lead. I liked Judge Campbell, and knew that he was to be trusted, but we had never been close.

He called to me from the library when I got downstairs. I went into the long, booklined room, and found him standing in front of the marble fireplace, a rolled newspaper in his hands. He was a spare, erect man with white hair and beard, and a voice that had the reaching delivery of the courtroom.

"I'm sorry to waken you, Tamson," he said.

"You didn't awaken me," I murmured.

"Good. Will you sit down for a moment?"

I was alarmed at his gravity. Surely a suddenly broken engagement couldn't cause him this much concern.

"My dear," he began slowly, "you must be aware by now, that wealth such as yours, can be a great burden at times?"

"I know, sir."

"And that your actions must be governed accordingly?"

"Of course."

"Wealth is always suspect, in the eyes of the masses, even when honestly come by, as yours is, and you must never give them a basis for scandal."

"Scandal!" My head came up with a jerk. "I don't know what you mean, Judge?"

"You must know that everything you do is of interest to outsiders, Tamson. Last night, there was a member of the press present at the Napier's—purely to cover the event for his social column. It was unfortunate that he was given the information before—others. If you had come to me last night—"

My head was in a whirl. "What story? I saw no gentleman from the press. I don't know what you are talking about!"

He came over to my chair and laid the newspaper in my lap, folded to the society page. With swimming sight I read the print below his pointing finger. To my fevered brain the letters seemed ten feet high.

NEW ENGLAND HEIRESS SPURNS FIANCE IN FAVOR OF SOUTHERN ARISTOCRAT

I read the story below with disbelieving eyes.

Miss Tamson Yorke, heiress to the great Yorke shipping fortune,

*last night broke off her engagement
to Captain John Markham, and
announced that she would marry
Mr. Breckenridge Rawlins, a planter
from South Carolina. The news
came as a complete surprise to Miss
Yorke's friends, and to the William
Napiers, at whose home a ball in
honor of Miss Yorke and Captain
Markham was in progress. Captain
Markham had no comment to make
regarding the breaking of his engagement under rather mysterious
circumstances.*

I stood up, my eyes hot as pokers in my
head. "How dare the newspapers print such a
thing? It's all a lie, a dastardly lie!"

The judge looked both relieved and
curious. "You did not break your engagement to Captain Markham?"

"I—not exactly. And I certainly never
told Mr. Rawlins, nor anyone else, that I
would marry him! It's all a complete false-
hood. Surely you can take the newspaper to
court over this?"

We were interrupted by the maid, Nan.
"Please, sir," she said, "there's a Mr. Rawlins
to see Miss Yorke."

I whirled to face the Judge. "Now," I
cried, "you can hear the truth for yourself."

He told Nan to show the caller into the
drawing room, and when she had gone, told
me, "I don't understand this, Tamson, but

perhaps you had better let me see Mr. Rawlins alone."

"No," I said quickly, "I want to speak to him first, before you see him. Please, it's best."

"I'm not sure that would be wise under the circumstances."

"Judge Campbell, I *must* talk to him alone first."

Something in my voice seemed to make him hesitate, "Very well, my dear. I shall wait in here. When you are ready you have only to call, or bring him into the library."

"Thank you," I said gratefully. "I will explain everything to you, I promise." I felt his eyes on me until I had shut the hall door behind me.

The drawing room was directly across the hall from the library, and Nan had carefully shut the big double doors, I paused a moment outside to straighten my shoulders and compose myself, but I could not lull the angry beating of my heart, or the flush I felt rising in my cheeks. Then I opened one half of the doors and stepped firmly into the room.

He was standing much as the Judge had been when I entered the library, in front of the fireplace, with his hands clasped behind his back. He seemed to loom much larger and wider than I remembered, and there was a faint sardonic smile on his dark face. The sight of it made the rage boil up inside me and I demanded:

"How dare you tell the newspapers that I have broken my engagement to John Markham, and that I am going to marry you!"

"It seemed fairly obvious last night that you had no intention of marrying John," he answered calmly. "As for the rest of it, that's why I've come at this inexcusable hour—to explain. You were too upset last night for me to even attempt to do so then. Will you sit down long enough to listen to what I have to say?"

I gave him a scathing look, but I sat down on the edge of a horsehair chair and folded my trembling hands in my lap. I had to find out what had happened last night after I fainted in the summerhouse, and just what was in the mind of this despicable man.

He sat down on a small sofa facing me. "I tried," he said, holding my eyes with his own, "to do you a favor last night."

"A favor!" My voice croaked with anger.

"Exactly. I did the only thing I could do under the circumstances. After you fainted and I couldn't bring you around, I decided to carry you out to my carriage and have Jason drive you home. I was halfway across the drive with you in my arms, when that reporter from the *Transcript* came along. He recognized you of course, but he couldn't see that your eyes were closed, your head was against my shoulder. Naturally he was suspicious, and I had to make up a story on the spot. I told him that you had just broken your engagement to John Markham, and promised to marry me. That we were on our way to a private celebration, and that if he would call here this afternoon, we would give him further details together."

"You had no right to tell him any such thing! There's not one word of truth in it!"

"I've given you a chance to save face," he said, "if I've done nothing else. You didn't intend to tell the world that Tamson Yorke plus the Yorke fortune had been jilted, did you?"

"It wouldn't matter—at least it would be better than this. It would be the truth."

"Hell!" he exploded, and it was the first time a man had ever sworn in my presence. "Haven't you learned yet that truth isn't worth the letters that spell it? Live by it and you'll be crucified, nailed to the cross by it. Do you think any of the people at that party, any of your so-called friends, any of the people who read the *Transcript* care a curse for what really happened last night? All they're interested in is whether the proud, rich, untouchable Miss Yorke can be brought down to their level where they can humiliate her. Are you going to hand them the stick to beat you with, when I've given you an out?" His eyes mocked me.

I had gotten to my feet. "If living a lie is to be the price of my pride and honor, I want no part of your magnanimous offer. When the reporter from the *Transcript* calls today, I will explain what really happened."

He stood up, one hand on the back of the sofa, and for a fleeting instant there was a look of admiration in his dark eyes.

"I believe," he said slowly, "that you would do just that but did you ever stop to think that there are others involved?"

My scorn whipped out at him, "If you think I care that you—"

He grinned at me. "I know you don't give a tinker's damn how this thing affects me; why should you? Nor do I imagine you feel too kindly towards Miss Napier. But how about Judge Campbell? The stark truth, if you insist upon using it, is bound to stir up a hornet's nest in the papers. Judge Campbell is your legal guardian and a man of importance. And what do you think it will do to the military career of Captain Markham?"

He was watching me closely as if everything depended on how I answered his last question. And I knew I couldn't answer it. I had lost John, my heart was stripped bare, but I knew even then that I could not ruin him. In a way, I felt, he had been helpless in his love for Lucy. At least he had not married me first and then told me. And neither he nor Lucy had any money. They had only John's army career to depend upon. I knew that officers were supposed to be, and act, like gentlemen. The whisper of any scandal could cripple John's advancement.

"Do you hate Markham that much?" asked my tormentor.

"No," I whispered. "I don't hate him."

I sank down on my chair again as the realization of the truth of what I had just admitted came home to me. I didn't hate John; I could never hate him. In spite of everything, he had given me the happiest moments I had ever known. I didn't want to hurt him, no matter what it cost me.

Breckenridge Rawlins had sat down again also, and was speaking in his drawling voice, slowly and carefully, as if he were addressing a child.

"I have a business proposition to make to you, Miss Yorke. Will you hear me out?"

I nodded dumbly. My world had crashed about me and I saw no way out. I knew I could never bring myself to tell Judge Campbell the truth. His sympathetic understanding, even if forthcoming, would be unbearable to me now. Somehow I had to handle this situation alone.

"You and I," Mr. Rawlins' voice went on, "have a great deal in common. We both need help out of our difficulties, but there is a matter of pride that makes it essential that we solve the problem ourselves. Am I right?"

I nodded again, though I was unwilling to agree with anything he said.

"You need to escape from an intolerable personal dilemma, and save your feminine pride. To do that you must have a husband, at least temporarily. I will be perfectly frank with you. I need money or the loan of it, for at least a year, in order to salvage my plantation and those dependent upon me. I came north to secure funds. I have failed to do so. But if you will consent to marry me and grant me the loan of enough money to put my plantation back on its feet, I can promise you a solution to your present problem plus complete freedom of your actions. Our marriage need only be a convenience on both sides. You will be mistress of a great house. At the end of a year, I am convinced, I will be able to repay the loan, and I will provide you with grounds for a divorce. I had not intended," he ended shortly, "to marry to obtain the money I need, but if I can serve you by doing so, I will be happy to oblige."

I was jolted out of my misery and self pity by his words.

"Serve me!" I cried. "I have no need of your services, thank you! I have no desire or intention of being married to you for an instant let alone a year. How dare you come to me with such a proposition?" I was sitting bolt upright, my hands clutching the arms of the chair.

He asked quietly, "Do you have a better solution to your predicament, Miss Yorke?" His smiled was the lazy confident one of the cat that has cornered the mouse, and can afford to play with it awhile before capturing it.

I realized that I should run to Judge Campbell and tell him the truth, all of it, but I knew that I would not. If this hateful man and his cold blooded proposition meant that John would be safe from recrimination and dishonor, then I knew that I must accept it.

He realized before I spoke that he had won, and I hated him for it.

"Very well," I said, barely above a whisper, "but only for one year. I will go south with you temporarily, but I will be free to go my own way. Perhaps I may travel for the rest of the year."

"Just as you wish," he said, and I was grateful that his voice was devoid of emotion.

I was empty of feeling myself when we went in to see Judge Campbell. And I was amazed at the smoothness with which my new fiance explained away my former reaction to him, in the presence of the Judge. A misunderstanding, a lovers' quarrel, had caused me to deny the newspaper report. But we had settled everything now, and wished to be married at once, since business called him back to his plantation. I was subdued in my responses, but I agreed with him.

We were married a week later, the Campbells insisting on holding the wedding in their home, and the press covered the story widely.

Before our wedding, I had settled a large sum of money on my husband to be, and Judge Campbell found it puzzling that I did not turn over all my holdings to Mr. Rawlins as was the custom. I explained that my father would have preferred I leave the bulk of my estate in his, the Judge's, capable hands until we knew exactly what we wanted to do. Banks in the south were not too stable as yet, and at best southern commerce was uncertain. He was forced to agree with the sense of this.

As a matter of form, I had invited Lucy and John as well as the Napiers, to our wedding, but they did not attend. John did send me a personal gift however, a chaste gold jewel box with a single initial T carved on top. The card that accompanied it said simply:

Be happy in the future, and remember only the happiness of the past.
John

I could not bring myself to destroy the card, and fitted it into the bottom of the blue satin lined box. I felt then that I had stored my youth and my love in that small gold coffin, never to be resurrected again.

My tears fell on the carved golden T and made it shine more brightly for an instant, before it blurred out of my sight.

3

Our honeymoon, we pretended to those who were interested, would be spent aboard the packet going to Charleston.

Once on board however, our pretenses vanished, and I was thankful that Mr. Rawlins (I could never think of him as Breckenridge), left me to my own resources.

We each had a large stateroom, and I made sure the connecting door was securely bolted on my side. My husband escorted me on deck and to and from meals, with scrupulous chivalry and attention, but I seldom saw him otherwise.

Lying on my bunk sleepless and wary, I would hear him come into his room in the early hours of the dawn. Sometimes he seemed to fall heavily against the furniture, at other times, I could hear him muttering in his sleep, but what he said I never knew.

I learned little about him on our trip. He

seldom mentioned his family, and when I asked about his plantation he answered me vaguely. "You'll see it soon enough and judge for yourself."

Thrown upon my own resources, I found that in spite of the odd circumstances, I was enjoying the voyage. I had traveled so seldom that everything was a new and invigorating experience to me. The ship was a luxurious one, with helpful stewards, excellent food, and always a new and fascinating vista.

I knew that my husband spent most of his time at the gaming tables, but I didn't care as long as he left me free to do as I pleased.

I found walking on deck in the early morning both invigorating and private. I was walking briskly one morning when I encountered another passenger.

He was an elderly man whom I had noticed dining alone the night before. He was small and neat, with gray hair and a gray goatee, and he affected an old-fashioned black cape.

"You're out very early, my dear," he said, with a deep southern accent and a sweeping bow.

I smiled at him. "Yes, it was stuffy in my cabin."

"Aren't you Mrs. Rawlins?" he asked politely.

I nodded.

"Mrs. Breckenridge Rawlins?"

"Yes."

"I'm Colonel Hues. I used to know your husband's father, though I haven't seen the family in some time. But I was often a guest at Harlequin."

"Harlequin?" I asked, puzzled.

"The Rawlins' plantation. The house is most historic—a landmark. I'm very thankful it was not badly damaged in the war."

I felt very foolish to admit that I knew nothing of Harlequin—the plantation or the house, so without further conversation I excused myself and returned to my cabin.

That day at lunch however, I asked my husband directly about his plantation.

He seemed reluctant to answer my question at first.

"Does the plantation have a name?" I asked innocently.

He hesitated a few moments before answering. "Yes, it's called Harlequin."

"What an unusual name. Did your family name it that?"

"No," he said slowly, "it's connected with family legend. It's a very old house."

"But I was talking about the plantation," I said.

He seemed relieved and dismissed that in a few words. "It was laid out in 1702."

"So early?"

"Yes. The family had come over from England much earlier. They were Royalists, and not too popular at that time."

"Mine were followers of Cromwell," I

said primly.

He seemed amused. "That was to be expected."

"Tell me about Harlequin. How large is it?"

"Only seven hundred acres now," he said bitterly. "It used to be seven thousand."

"I'm sorry," I said automatically.

He glanced sharply at my face and then said, "No need to be; my ancestors sold it off or gambled it away. But the land could have saved them if they'd only known it. It can still save Harlequin House."

"You speak of the house as if it were a separate entity."

"It is. Harlequin is the original Rawlins' manor house that was built in England in 1540. A great many historical events took place inside its walls. When my ancestors came to this country, they had the house torn down, shipped here and re-assembled. And so of course it retains its traditional name." A dark brooding look came over his face and he glanced at me almost in anger.

"I sense that you don't like to talk about it," I said quietly.

He answered me savagely, "Harlequin means everything to me!"

I did not ask him any more questions.

We landed in Charleston very early the next morning, and I had never seen a place more fascinating or picturesque.

I had always heard that it was the least American city in the United States, and from

the first moment I was utterly charmed by it.
Coming as I did from the north, I was
delighted with the mellow aged look of pink
and mauve walls, caused no doubt by the
lingering humid heat and heavy tropical
rains. I made out palm trees, yuccas and
palmettos, and beneath them on sandy
street corners, the knots of indolent Negroes, the women wearing gaily colored
turbans and full calico skirts. Yet I sensed,
under the surface quiet of the place, a
primitive and violent current.

Jason, my husband's coachman who
had driven us in Boston, had come south
with us on the packet, and he appeared
shortly on the wharf driving a rather old
carriage and two matched gray horses.

"Is it far to Harlequin?" I asked as my
husband helped me down the gangplank.

"Some little ways. But if you're too tired
to go on today, we can stay over in Charleston."

"No," I said quickly, "I want to get there
as soon as possible."

He seemed relieved, and we were soon
traveling down the sandy roads. He pointed
out the places of interest as we passed, the
Dock Street Theater, where in 1812 an
orchestra made up of French refugees from
Santo Domingo had been extremely popular, the colorful sidewalk cafes, the library
containing over 4000 volumes, the Jockey
Club, the mansions and churches designed
by Sir Christopher Wren. Beneath giant

oaks, I could catch a glimpse of graceful Georgian doorways, fluted columns and long shaded galleries. The white men who passed us on the road had the look of English squires, booted and spurred and mounted on superb horses. Several of them nodded to us and doffed their hats in deference to me.

The heat was oppressive, tropical in its thick clinging intensity, and my handkerchief and clothing were damp in a short time. Oddly, the heat seemed to have no effect on my husband. He slumped back in his seat, the brim of his hat well down over his narrowed eyes, and seemed so unapproachable that I attempted only the briefest conversation with him while we shared a basket lunch during the noon hour.

It was very late in the afternoon when we left the road and turned in at a huge stone arch where two small Negro boys stood holding the tall wrought iron gates. They bobbed their curly heads as we swept through, and I heard the gates clang shut behind us.

From my parched throat I asked, "Is this Harlequin?"

"Yes," replied my husband in a sardonic tone. "Welcome to Harlequin, Mrs. Rawlins."

I was still startled to hear myself called that, but never more so than when my husband said it. It gave me the eerie feeling of performing in a play with him, for which neither of us was prepared.

I leaned forward, but all I could see was the avenue of immense live oaks festooned with gray moss that met in an arch over the drive, all but shutting out the light. It was rather like moving underwater in a fetid cavern. We seemed to go on for ages, although I learned later it was only two miles from the gate to Harlequin House. My husband was leaning forward now too, his muscular hands clasped between his knees, an intense, almost wary, look on his dark face.

We swept into the circular drive and I saw my future home for the first time.

The immediate thought that crossed my mind was that it was not at all like the graceful mansions I had admired along our route. This was a great brick pile that seemed to soar upwards from its square base, to its numerous decorative chimneys. It seemed Tudor in style, though I was no expert on architecture, but I saw high gables and counted at least two bay windows with leaded panes. It was grim and overwhelming by its very gigantic size, and was not my idea of a welcoming southern plantation house. It seemed as brooding and secretive as my husband, and for the first time I realized why it meant so much to him. They were alike, this monolithic pile of ancient brick, and the strange man I had married.

He held out his hand to help me down from the carriage and I realized that it was dusk. At the same moment the huge iron-studded oak door opened and three female figures emerged. In the fading light I could only make out that one was middle-aged, one young, and the last was a very tall black woman.

Mr. Rawlins led me up the four wide shallow steps, straight to the middle-aged woman. "Aunt Samantha, may I present my wife, Tamson. My dear, this is my aunt Samantha Girole, my late mother's sister."

She came forward, a small, dark, plump woman, with kind but worried dark eyes, and taking my face between her soft palms kissed me quickly on the cheek.

"My child, we are so delighted that Breckenridge has married at last. Welcome to Harlequin, my dear, dear Tamson!"

I had come from a family that did not often show affection outwardly, and I was embarrassed, but Aunt Samantha seemed to mean it so genuinely that I was touched.

The young girl standing beside her was another proposition altogether. She was perhaps fifteen or sixteen, tiny, as were many southern women, I was to find out, with pale blonde hair and narrow green eyes, looking at me now like a kitten about to hiss and spit. She was pretty in a delicate Dresden doll sort of way, but I could feel the venom in her glance as our eyes met, and my husband must have sensed it too, for he said quickly:

"Tamson, this is Persis Girole, my cousin, the daughter of my mother's brother.

Persis, your Cousin Tamson."

She lowered her eyes and curtsied very gracefully, but I could see the tension in her narrow hands where they grasped her spotless but rather worn dimity skirt. "Welcome, Cousin Tamson." It was little more than a murmur.

Both my husband and the tall black woman gave her a cold speculative look, and the girl at once stammered, "Welcome to your new home, Cousin Tamson," with more warmth, but I knew she did not mean it. For some reason Persis hated me.

"This," said my husband with the first smile I had seen on his face since our arrival, "is Honore Delacroix. She is the mainstay of Harlequin."

Most Negroes, I had heard, were not given last names when introduced, so this woman must be something special.

She bowed and smiled. She seemed older than Miss Samantha, but I couldn't be sure. She was tall, erect, spare, with a coin-thin profile that was arresting in its beauty and proud bearing. Her skin was a light bisque brown. She wore a neat white dress and apron, a block watered turban, and a matching kerchief around her neck. She looked a very regal figure, and for some reason seemed to dominate all of us. I did not know much about Negroes, except what I had read or been told, but Honore Delacroix did not seem to fit into any category with which I was familiar. I had never expected to find a woman of her type in the south, and it seemed for an instant when I met her unflinching black eyes, that she was the real mistress of Harlequin, and that she alone could admit me. She did so now with another gracious bow saying simply, "Madame, I welcome you to Harlequin."

My husband seemed pleased. He smiled at Honore and then at me, and led me inside. We parted in the huge oval hall that contained a great circular staircase that seemed to wind upwards into oblivion. Honore led me silently up the stone stairs to my rooms while the others remained below—for a family conference, I supposed.

Upstairs the halls were long and broad. There were dim family portraits lining the walls, and a good many excellent landscapes that looked valuable. Yet there were unmistakable marks of poverty and wear. The carpets were threadbare, paint was falling from the walls in spots and there were marks of dry rot and roof leaks.

Honore ushered me into a luxurious suite made up of a large bedroom, sitting room and dressing room. She explained that my husband would occupy a similar suite beyond, and that they were connected by the dressing room door.

When Honore left me to fetch hot water, I examined my own bedroom with interest. It was paneled in very old pearwood, a large square room with a bay window overlooking the front drive and the avenue of oaks. Here, as in the hallways, the carpet was badly faded and worn, as were the dark green velvet drapes. The furniture was Jacobean in design, obviously authentic and very old and quite overpowering in its carved immensity. The huge covered bed with posts as large as small casks, was high with a step-stool to mount to it. The bed had been freshly made and the counterpane of green velvet neatly turned back. From the green velvet canopy hung a filmy mesh of new white mosquito netting, also folded back. There was an immense carved *armoire* against one wall, a desk, a deep-lidded chest, and in front of the stone fireplace, two winged chairs covered in worn pale green brocade. One of them had a ladies' footstool in front of it. There was a silver vase of roses on a small table near the window seat that filled the bay window, and a bookcase near the bed containing a few calf bound volumes that looked very old and unused.

I peeked into the dressing room, and found one wall was fitted with various closets and cupboards, while the other wall formed a lengthy dressing table with a large, damp-spotted mirror above.

Honore returned a moment later accompanied by two stout Negro girls carrying cans of water. She unearthed a hip bath from one of the closets and set it up in the dressing room. She said, "Jason is bringing your luggage. Do you wish me to unpack for you, madame?"

"Yes, please, Honore," I said gratefully, for I had not realized how the heat had sapped my vitality, "but I'm afraid you will find everything terribly wrinkled."

"I will take care of that, madame. Will you tell me what you wish to wear tonight?"

"There's a blue moire," I said, "that should be the least wrinkled." It was rather a heavy material for such a hot night, but it was pale in color and cut low. "And thank you, Honore," I added.

She inclined her regal turbaned head as she helped me undress, and supervised the temperature of the bath water. She left me with a pile of soft fluffy towels, a new bar of homemade soap delicately scented with lemon verbena, which she said she had made, and began to unpack the contents of my dressing case, laying them out on the dressing table. She glanced longest at the gold jewel case John had given me. Before she left again, she showed me a bell pull in the corner and asked me to ring when I was finished and she would return with my gown, help me to dress, and assist me with my hair. I thanked her again and sank down gratefully in the hot scented water. I had never enjoyed a bath more.

When I had finished I put on a filmy silken wrapper Honore had unpacked for me, and sat down before the dressing table mirror. I patted my skin generously with rose water to cool it after the hot bath. Somewhere outside I heard a mockingbird trill.

But inside the house itself there was not a sound. I finished my toilet and rang for Honore.

From the windows I could see that it was quite dark now, and I wondered what the rest of the night held in store for me in this strange, brooding mansion, with its ancient walls so steeped in history. I had always felt that houses had an aura, a personality of their own, and I tried to think how Harlequin House had impressed me when I first entered it. All I had seen of it so far of course was the great entry hall, and the long corridor above leading to my own rooms. But thinking back I realized that there had been a distinct feeling of some kind as I entered the flagged front hall with my husband. I frowned into the mirror trying to recall what it had been.

At the same instant my eye was attracted by a faint movement in the wall behind me. Had one of the doors swung slightly open? My eyes moved quickly over them but I couldn't be sure. It was old wood; perhaps one of the catches hadn't been fastened securely, or some faint night breeze had blown one momentarily ajar. But I remembered Honore very carefully shutting those she had opened. The two Negro girls had merely emptied their water cans. I shrugged and began to brush my hair with long strokes of the silver backed brush. The silver brought out an answering glint in the opposite wall; something was winking and shining there. Annoyed, this time I turned fully around on the padded stool and stared at the fitted doors. There was one that was not as tightly closed as the others, or it was warped and did not fit as snugly into its frame.

I got up and went across to it. It was one of the larger doors. I tugged at the handle but it did not yield readily. Perturbed now, I gave it all my strength and it flew open with a protesting squeak, as if personally affronted. I peered inside. It was only a closet as I had surmised, smelling musty and unused. It was completely empty. I touched the walls but they were solid with no cracks anywhere. I was just deciding that it was merely the shine of my brush in the mirror that had caught a reflection from the lamp when I heard Honore enter.

I heard her footsteps halt abruptly, and turned towards her with a smile. The smile died on my lips. Her face was ashen under its ordinary bisque shade.

Her black eyes had a dazed, distant look, as if she were viewing something inwardly that both frightened and immobilized her. Her lips formed words but no sound came forth.

"Honore!" I cried, alarmed now myself. I went to her and shook the arm that held my blue moire dress. "Honore!"

At last her attention seemed to return to me from a great distance. She said as if puzzled, "Madame?"

"You—you must have had an attack of

some kind. Won't you sit down if you don't feel well?"

She shook her head, vigorously now, and her eyes and complexion were normal again. "It is nothing, madame, now and then I am subject to such things, but they pass quickly. Here is your gown—no wrinkles, you see?" She smiled and arranged the dress on a hanger. "Now we will arrange your hair, no?"

She seemed to think in French, although her English was faultless, and I was curious about her background. I felt however that this was not the time to question her, but something in this room had frightened her into a trancelike state. I suddenly felt a strong desire to leave the place myself. I knew, however, that fear was contagious, and lectured myself severely on the subject while Honore did my hair in a modish *chignon,* but it was no use. I still disliked being in the room. It seemed to my imagination that unseen eyes stared at us from the cupboard wall, and the mirror was so ancient and spotted that it was hard to tell where reality began and imagination left off.

"Madame looks exquisite." She gave the words the French pronunciation as she stepped back, and I was foolishly pleased.

I got up from the stool and glanced at my full length reflection in the mirror. My pale robin's egg blue gown fitted my shoulders, bust and slim waist to perfection. Honore had bound my *chignon* with dark lavender ribbons that matched the necklace of amethysts I had chosen to wear. It was a Yorke family heirloom, with drop earrings to match, that had belonged to my great-grandmother, and that Judge Campbell had insisted be insured at a very high rate. The Yorke women had never possessed a great many jewels, as their Puritan tastes were simple, but those that they did own were faultless and beautifully mounted.

Someone knocked at the sitting room door, and Honore went to answer it. I heard my husband's voice asking if I was ready.

I swept out at once to meet him. He stood just inside the door, attired in evening clothes. His face was as masklike as always, but I saw something move in his dark eyes before he narrowed the lids in a way that made me think of a hooded falcon.

"You look very lovely," he said, more I felt for Honore's benefit than mine.

"Thank you," I replied politely, for the same reason.

He offered me his arm, and led me rather thoughtfully down to dinner.

4

The dining room was large and oval in shape, with walls covered in faded blue damask, large oak furniture, and an immense carved sideboard holding a great English silver service.

The servants were soft footed and efficient, and the meal more than satisfying: shrimp bisque, terrapin, roasted chicken with fluffy rice, beaten biscuits, and pecan pie. The coffee though, when we had it later in the vast drawing room with its giant empty fireplaces at either end, tasted of the chicory that had come into use out of necessity during the war.

It was a rather strained and silent quarter of an hour, as both Persis and my husband seemed preoccupied with their own thoughts. Aunt Samantha tried bravely on her own to keep up a running fire of small talk, and I did my best to respond, but as I knew none of the people or places she spoke of, and certainly nothing of plantation life, it was a poor exchange.

When we had finished coffee, my husband excused himself to go to his study and speak with his overseer. I was to learn that this was his usual custom.

Persis also excused herself and went over to the large square rosewood piano in the corner and began to play a Chopin waltz both well and with surprising feeling.

I mentioned the fact to Aunt Samantha.

"Poor child, she was at school in New Orleans, at the Ursiline Convent, and was one of their most promising music students. But since the end of the war, with hard times upon us, there was nothing that Breckenridge could do but bring her here. Her father, my brother Lige, was killed at Vicksburg, and her mother died shortly afterwards—of a broken heart I do believe."

"Were you here, at Harlequin, during the war?" I asked.

Her eyes grew dark with painful memory. "Yes, part of the time. My dear, it was terrible. The constant fear, and hardly any food, and then troops were billeted here and I had to leave. I stayed in Charleston with friends, but I worried so about Harlequin. And when the war was over, there was only Breckenridge and myself and Persis left to come back and pick up the pieces."

She was weeping softly, and I felt very sorry for her. I knew now that my husband had married me not only to save Harlequin, but to

protect the two women he held dear, and I did
not feel so unkindly towards him. I could see
for myself how badly money was needed to
repair the house inside, but I could only guess
how much would be needed to sow crops and
restore the rest of the plantation. I supposed
that the place was short handed, and up to
now my husband had probably had no money
with which to pay wages. Slavery was no
more, for which I was grateful, but I knew that
the whole economy of the agricultural south
had been dependent on free labor, and it
would take decades to change.

Upon one subject however, Aunt Samantha and I found a congenial interest: Harlequin
House. I had been able to find out very little
about its history from my husband, but
Samantha Girole, even if she had not been
born a Rawlins, knew all about its colorful
background and was delighted to talk about it.

"My own maternal family, the Malots,"
said Aunt Samantha, "were Huguenot French,
and actually came to this country before the
Rawlins, though I must say we were never as
well off." She smiled and touched my wrist
lightly with her black lace fan. "My dear, the
Rawlins were Royalists, and had to flee when
they beheaded poor King Charles. But they
managed to get away with most of their
fortune, and old Lord Geoffrey had Harlequin
House torn down and shipped here and re-
assembled. He owned over seven thousand
acres here at the time, it has dwindled terribly
of course. Bad investments, expenses and—"

She hesitated.

"And gambling?" I asked boldly.

She flushed and then said, "Yes, I am sorry to say the Rawlins men were always sporting men. I hope that you will try to understand, Tamson, that it is something in the blood, as my dear sister Emilie had to come to understand."

I changed the subject deliberately seeing that she was becoming upset again. "You started to tell me about Harlequin House itself."

Aunt Samantha fanned herself languidly in the sultry heat that seemed to fill even this vaulted chamber. "Harlequin House was built in the latter Fourteen Hundreds. The family was in royal favor at the time and owned a large property in Sussex. Many famous people visited Harlequin, including, I am told, Henry the Seventh and his son, Henry the Eighth. Originally the house had one hundred rooms, but in the Fifteen Hundreds one entire wing was destroyed by fire and never reconstructed." She seemed suddenly to lose interest in the past history of the house and said instead, "Tomorrow I will show you over the entire place. After all you are now mistress of Harlequin." She took up a small velvet drawstring bag she had carried in from dinner, opened it, and drew out a large ring of keys.

"You must take charge of these now, Tamson. They are the keys to the entire house. Breckenridge has had to order many of the rooms shut up—the expense you know—but either Honore or I will show you which ones. You won't find it difficult once you have been over the house."

"But, Aunt Samantha," I said, "I know nothing about running a house. I've been at school, like Persis, a boarder since my parents died, and I wouldn't know how to start. Please, won't you keep the keys for now? Perhaps, with your help and Honore's, I may be able to do better in time."

She smiled at me but her brown eyes were determined. She took my hand and pressed the ring of keys firmly into my palm, closing my unwilling fingers over them.

"My dear, every young bride feels inadequate. It is hard for any of us to accept responsibility willingly. But I assure you that Breckenridge will expect you to keep these yourself. Rest assured Honore and I will help you in every way, but the mistress of a plantation like Harlequin has a duty and responsibility as great as her husband's. You will learn quickly, I am sure. It will not be as easy as it was in my sister's time before the war, when the slaves—" she paused looking suddenly conscience stricken. "Oh, dear, I didn't mean to bring up that subject; do forgive me."

"It's all right, Aunt Samantha," I said. "Actually I know very little about the war, for I was at school, and I'm afraid political issues are another thing with which I am unfamiliar. Being from the north, I was brought up to believe that owning and selling people was wrong. I am sorry there had to be a war over it."

"Thank you, my dear," she said faintly. "Breckenridge has told us all we must never mention the war in this house again. We are to forget all about it and start our lives over, but sometimes one is inclined to live in the past." Her voice had grown so low I could hardly hear it.

At that moment another voice at my elbow said, "Don't let her play on your sympathies about the dear, dead past."

My husband was standing there in the shadows of the dimly lighted room, a sheaf of papers in one hand, and a scowl on his dark face.

"Breckenridge!" Aunt Samantha's cheeks had gone white. "My dear, I was only trying—"

"To recapture the past again," he finished for her angrily, "I told you the past is dead and buried for us in this house. Do you understand?"

"Yes," she whispered.

I was suddenly furious with him for browbeating his gracious little aunt. He was a demon even in his own house. I was very glad that ours was a marriage of convenience only, and that in a year I would be free of him and Harlequin forever.

He turned to me and said politely, "I would like to see you for a moment in my study, Tamson. You should know about certain matters pertaining to the plantation."

I rose, an angry flag of color in my own cheeks, but I decided to have it out with him in private. Persis had stopped playing and was staring at us, and Aunt Samantha held a handkerchief to her eyes, her head bowed. It was not a reassuring beginning of my life at Harlequin House.

I followed my husband from the drawing room, across the hall to an alcove under the stairs where he threw open a door and stood aside to let me pass.

This was purely a workroom, I saw at a glance, rather small, furnished simply with a desk, chairs, bookcases and some extra wide shelves behind the desk that seemed to hold ledgers and what looked like stacks of maps. There was a worn horsehair sofa, and two wing chairs flanking the small stone fireplace. As we entered, a man arose from one of the chairs. He was tall, rather young, with corn-colored hair, almost white brows and lashes, and a bony, freckled face. It was a hard face with a long wire-thin mouth, and light blue eyes as unwinking as china marbles.

"Tamson," said my husband, "this is Sam Forbes, the overseer. Sam, Mrs. Rawlins."

I nodded and he bowed very low from the waist.

"My honor, ma'am." His voice was grave and respectful but there was something in his light eyes that mocked me. His greeting reminded me of a schoolboy giving required politeness to a teacher.

My husband seemed not to notice. He

laid down the sheaf of papers he had been carrying and handed me into one of the wing chairs. Forbes remained standing, even when my husband sat down behind the desk. I noted he did not invite the man to sit down again, which I found strange, but then so many things at Harlequin puzzled me.

My husband addressed me directly. "When I am away, you will of course be in charge here. I want to put no more burden on you than necessary, but there will be certain matters that you must handle from this office. I will leave you full instructions."

"But," I began, "I know nothing about—"

My husband would not let me finish: his eyes were hard on mine. "You are the only one here capable of doing it," he told me, "and Forbes here, will help you."

"My pleasure, ma'am," said Forbes.

"You're not going away?" I asked my husband.

"Not at once, but I must see what extra help I can get. We are badly in need of it if we are to get the fields ready for the new crops I've planned to put in. I also hope to get some good mares and a blooded stallion, to start our stable again. We lost all our horses during the war," he ended briefly.

"Some of the finest stock in the south, ma'am," said Forbes, and I did not like the faint note of satisfaction that I thought I detected under his tones of polite regret.

"Very well," I said. "I will do my best."

My husband's glance held a sudden relief

and respect.

"Thank you, my dear. These"—he touched the papers on his desk—"are outstanding debts which must be paid before we can proceed to build up Harlequin again and secure the necessary credits."

"But why must you take on creditors again?" I asked. "Pay these accounts and whatever else is needed to put the plantation on a sound footing again."

Both he and Forbes gave me an indulgent smile.

"My dear Tamson, that is not good business. One never puts all one's cash into a venture. It is financed instead and the cash kept for emergencies. Having cleared our debts I can expect to get unlimited credit again. Forbes will issue you written requests for the funds he will require for supplies, salaries and farm needs. You will in turn give him the monies needed from this office, filing his requests and signed receipts. I just wanted to make it clear to both of you in my presence. Very well, you may go, Forbes."

"Yes, sir." Forbes made me that sweeping bow again and left the room.

Mr. Rawlins got up and began to pace the room on his long legs. "I dislike bringing you into all this; my mother never had to be concerned with such things. But this is a new and different era we are living in."

"I don't mind," I said, "if it's only for a short while."

"Good. I'll try not to be away for more

than a few weeks. I know that you said you might wish to travel, but I had hoped you might like Harlequin enough to remain here. I realize I have no right to expect it—to ask it of you, but things are really in a bad way here. You've met Aunt Samantha and Persis. Neither of them is capable of carrying on even with Forbes' help."

"You put a great deal of faith in Forbes, don't you?"

"Yes, of course. His father worked for my Uncle Jules Girole. He's a good overseer. Don't you like him?"

"I don't know; I've just met him."

His dark eyes narrowed. "But a woman's intuition is notoriously correct. What is it you dislike about him?"

"I don't think he's as subservient as he appears," I said.

He laughed. "Few hirelings are. But he knows crops and how to work the hands. His personality isn't important."

"If you are satisfied," I said, "we should consider the matter settled. After all, Harlequin is your concern."

He hesitated a moment longer studying my face, then went back to his desk. "There are two men I want you to meet tomorrow," he said presently, "the family lawyer, Virgil Jessup, and our banker, Pierre Legros, at whose bank I intend to deposit—our funds."

"They are your funds," I told him crisply. "The settlement was part of our bargain."

His face colored, but he said steadily,

"While we remain married, they must be considered *our* funds. I am also going to make out a will in your favor, with bequests for Aunt Samantha and Persis, of course."

I stared at him in astonishment. "But why bother to do that? I am independently wealthy, and in a year—"

"I know," he cut me off harshly, "But a year can be a long time. It's impossible to tell what might happen."

"Then you would expect me to make a will in your favor?"

He smashed his fist down on the desk top and shouted, "I'd expect and want no such damned thing! I told you in the beginning, all I wanted was enough money to save Harlequin and put it on its feet again. Well, I've got that. I want nothing more, is that clear? But it's only sense for me to make out a will insuring its safety for as long as I can."

"And after we're divorced?"

"Naturally, I will make other arrangements."

I said nothing more, but again his mood changed.

"How do you like Harlequin, what you've seen of it?"

"It's very unusual, and so large it overwhelms me."

"But how does it impress you, personally?" he was watching my face closely with his hard, dark gaze.

"I don't quite know," I mused. "I suppose I feel that a house this old, that has seen eras change, has secrets it can never divulge."

"That's very perceptive of you, Tamson. They are the same thoughts I had about it as a child. But make no mistake about it, Harlequin House has a will and a temper of its own still. This house has always dominated the Rawlins, it has never been the other way around." His voice grew quieter and at the same time more intense. "It's as if we live in it by tolerance rather than right. Can you understand that?"

"Yes," I said, "I suppose much the same feeling comes over royal families who replace each other in historic places; the building itself has stored up so much more living and so many more memories than they will ever know in a lifetime."

"Exactly. I hope you won't find living here, however briefly, too trying. I don't mean your stay to be burdensome or—unhappy. You must tell me at once if anything displeases you."

"Of course," I said, getting to my feet. "And now if you don't mind, I would like to go to my room. I am rather tired."

"Forgive me; of course you must be worn out." He rose to see me to the door.

A few minutes later I was in my room and Honore had arrived as if by magic to help me undress. I still had a strange reluctance to use the dressing room, but Honore showed no signs of her former trance-like fear. She chatted brightly as she brushed and braided my hair and tied the ends with fresh pink ribbons to match my silk nightdress and robe.

"Miss Samantha says we will show you all of Harlequin House tomorrow, madame. You have the keys, no?"

I nodded.

"Good. The house is not what it was before the war, but even General Sherman, when he came through, did not destroy Harlequin as he did so many of the other houses. Even *he* recognized greatness when he saw it, or perhaps he felt the presence of other military commanders who have walked its halls."

"You know the history of the house, Honore?"

"Yes, madame. My family has served Harlequin since it was built," her head came up proudly.

When I had mounted the steps to the great canopied bed, she blew out all the lamps leaving a single lighted candle on a bedside table within reach.

"Goodnight, madame."

"Goodnight, Honore."

"Should you need me, ring there by the door. I will not be long in coming."

"Thank you," I said. I was really very tired, and wished she would leave, but she took her time adjusting the mosquito net. When she had finished, she stood for a moment gazing at me.

"Madame, should you hear any sounds in the night that seem strange to you, do not be alarmed. Such an ancient house as this has many unaccountable noises."

"Of course," I said, "and they won't bother me in the least, I assure you. I'm so tired I could sleep through an earthquake."

At the door she paused and spoke quietly over her shoulder. "You know, madame, this has always been the bridal suite at Harlequin. Many brides have slept in this very bed in which you are sleeping." With that she went out and closed the door softly behind her.

I leaned forward and blew out the candle, not bothering to unfasten the netting to do so. At once all the night sounds came in through the partially shuttered windows. Honore had insisted the windows could not be left wide open due to the miasma, so even though there was a full moon, only a filtered light sifted into the room, picking out highlights here and there—picture frame, a corner of the dresser, the upper panel of the dressing room door.

Outside I heard a catbird cry, and some small animal, prey no doubt to a larger one, gave a quick strangled scream and was still. I could hear the angry buzz of the hungry mosquitos outside my net, but Honore had arranged it so expertly that not one got inside.

I lay for a few moments listening to the sounds inside the house itself. They were made up of the expected noises of an old house, the creaking and settling as the temperature altered slightly, the scratch of mice between the old walls, the rasp of hinges as a nearby door opened and closed. Then I lost track of the sounds and fell into a deep sleep.

I was dreaming of a procession of brides all in nightdresses, each of a different vintage, coming up and down the steps to the bed, when I was suddenly awake.

I couldn't hear anything unusual except the thudding of my own heart. I had no idea how long I had slept. The moonbeams were not in quite the same places as before, so I must have been asleep some little while. The angry buzzing of the insects outside the net had lessened too, and the air was a trifle cooler, though I was damp with perspiration. Did the humid heat never let up day or night, I wondered? I was very thirsty. There was drinking water in a carafe on the washstand I knew, and I decided to brave the mosquitoes to get it.

I pushed back the sheet that covered me, and opened a slit in the net just wide enough to let me slip through. At once the insects began to nip at my arms and face. I slapped them away, while my feet found the steps and I climbed quickly down to the floor. I could see quite well in the filtered light and didn't bother to light the candle which would only have attracted more insects. I reached the washstand and gulped down two glasses of tepid water. Then I poured some in the bowl and rinsed my hands and face. Cooler, and more refreshed, I had turned back towards the bed when I was aware of a sound coming from the dressing room. Then I saw with a shock that the door to that room was standing wide open. I knew Honore had left it closed. My bedroom door of course had not been locked, so someone might have slipped in while I slept and opened it. I was suddenly angry and humiliated at the thought that Mr. Rawlins might have stood watching me while I slept.

I called out instantly: "Who is there?"

There was no answer, and not light enough to see into the dressing room, which had no windows itself.

"Who is it?" I cried again.

I could still hear the sound, a gentle swishing, as if someone in a long gown were moving back and forth, the same sounds I would have made, I thought, if I had been dressing. I even thought I heard a door open and shut, perhaps one of the cupboard doors. It was preposterous, as if someone was hoping to scare me. But who could it be? Persis was the only one I could think of childish enough to try such a thing. If she disliked me, all well and good—but this was a foolish and rude way of showing it. I made my way to the dresser where I knew there was a lamp. When I had it alight I strode, angry now, into the dressing room.

There was no one there. Nothing. I glanced in the mirror and saw only the spotted reflection of my own angry face. But my anger was giving way to puzzlement. Had I dreamed it all? Was it just an aftermath of my dream of the parade of brides in nightdresses climbing up and down the steps to the bed?

I examined the wall of cupboards. Every drawer, every door was closed tightly, except the one that I had noticed earlier that seemed sprung from its frame. I touched it and found it slightly damp. I held my fingers under the light.

There was something on them. Red. Sticky.

I felt horror rise up in me as I dropped the lamp, smashing it.

Then in the darkness of the ancient little room I began to scream.

5

I don't know when I became aware of voices and lights and people around me. I suppose it was when someone began to shake me violently and I felt hands like an eagle's talons biting into the flesh of my arms. My head jerked back and forth like a broken doll's, and a harsh voice commanded:

"Stop it! For God's sake stop it, Tamson!"

The tone of the voice seemed to affect me more than the words, for my mouth closed and silence covered the little room like a thick blanket.

Startled, I looked up into my husband's furious, and at the same time wary, dark eyes. When he saw that I was aware of him he demanded, "What in the name of heaven happened to you?"

I struggled free of his hurting grasp and rubbed my numb arms. "Something—frightened me," I stammered. Even now nothing was quite clear to me.

"Obviously, but what was it? You can see there is nothing here but a smashed lamp, which you must have dropped."

I nodded.

"Then what—"

"Breckenridge, do let her tell it in her own way," begged Aunt Samantha. "Go on, my dear."

"I—I got up for a glass of water," I said, avoiding my husband's cold, disapproving glance, "when I heard something in here."

"Heard something?"

"Yes—a sound like someone dressing, a woman—there was the sound of a skirt or of cloth, swishing. And I thought I heard a closet door close."

My three companions stared at me blankly, for besides my husband, there were only Aunt Samantha and Persis present, the latter wearing a patched satin robe. I remember thinking absently that I must get her a new one soon.

"Tamson, this is idiotic," said my husband. "You were tired, slept poorly and no doubt had a vivid dream. When you got up for a drink you probably heard a mouse or something behind the walls, saw some sort of reflection in the mirror when you walked in here—no doubt your own—and became hysterical."

"I have never been hysterical in my life," I said through my teeth, loathing him. "I tell you I *heard* someone or something in here, a

distant sound of clothing rustling. I *do* know
the difference between the sound of mice and
of cloth moving." I glanced at the connecting
door that Honore had said led to my husband's
suite beyond.

He saw my look and stepped forward with
a grim expression, to try it. It had been bolted
on my side. He had to work hard with the
rusted bolt before he could push it back. A sift
of dust fell down as he threw open the door.

"You can see for yourself this hasn't been
opened in years. As a matter of fact these
particular rooms have not been in use since
my parents died. It was only because it is
considered the Bridal Suite, that Aunt Samantha persuaded me it was the proper one to use.
But there are a great many rooms in this
house, so we can move to another suite
tonight if you like."

I realized I must appear foolish and giddy
in their eyes. Persis wore a smug expression
on her young face. All my old New England
pride rose to the surface.

"No, that won't be necessary."

"Do you want someone to stay here with
you till morning?"

"No," I said coldly, detesting him, as I
watched him leave the room with Persis. Aunt
Samantha paused by the doorway.

"This has upset you, my child. I'm going
to send Honore to you with a cool drink and
one of her sleeping draughts. She's a most
efficient healer you know, just as her mother
was."

"No thank you," I said, "I'll have no trouble going to sleep now." I was not at all sure of this, but I spoke firmly.

"I insist," said Aunt Samantha, and there was an odd look of determination in her usually soft brown eyes. She repeated the words, "I insist."

I left all the lamps burning when she had gone, in spite of the cloud of insects it attracted, but to avoid their vicious attacks I climbed back into bed and fastened the netting around me. Seated in the middle of my big bed, reaction suddenly set in. I began to tremble and then suddenly to weep, in great wracking sobs that shook the bed. I did not hear Honore enter the room. But I felt a hand laid gently on my arm, and a voice said soothingly, "Here, madame, drink this. It will make you feel better."

I glanced up into Honore's face. She was holding out a glass to me through the small section of parted netting. The glass pressed into my palm felt cool and tinkled with ice.

"Drink it, madame. I know all about what happened and you are not to worry. We will talk in the morning."

For some reason I trusted this woman more than anyone else in this strange house. I drank the cool fruit mixture gratefully, even greedily. If there was any medication in it, I did not taste it. Then as I lay back on my pillow, Honore took the glass from me and fitted the net back in place as deftly as she did all things.

"I will sit in the room until you are asleep.

Please do not be afraid. Rest now."

I closed my eyes obediently, and in no time I seemed to drift off on a cloud of peace and comfort.

The next thing I knew, mockingbirds woke me singing outside my window. The room was fairly cool and shadowed, and I felt languid but refreshed. I had no idea what time it was; oddly, the room had no clock—perhaps because it had not been used in such a long time. I would have to ask Honore for one.

As if she appeared in answer to my thought, she tapped and entered the room, followed by a little maid carrying a tray.

"In view of madame's restless night, Miss Samantha ordered breakfast in bed for you this morning."

"How nice," I said, suddenly aware that I was famished. It must indeed be late. "What time is it?" I asked as Honore helped me into a frilly bed jacket.

"Only ten, madame. But Mr. Rawlins breakfasted early, as usual, in order to ride out with Forbes. And the ladies also had breakfast in bed today, though they don't as a rule. The master said he would return at midday, and you are to go to Croix with him."

The little maid placed the tray on my lap and then withdrew. Honore remained, opening the shutters to let in the sunshine that was already hot.

"Where is Croix?" I asked, enjoying the fresh strawberries and cream, the hot biscuits and nicely poached egg.

"It is our nearest town of any size, madame, where the master does most of his business."

"But I should think Charleston would be the most logical place for that."

"No, madame. Croix suffices, and it is much closer."

"I see." I was wiping my fingers on the fine but worn linen napkin when I saw the stains on their tips, dried brown now. Suddenly all the horror of the previous night came back to me. I held my hands straight out, as if to keep them away from me, and the tray toppled and fell from the bed with a fearful clatter. I jumped from the bed to the floor.

"Madame! What is it?" cried Honore.

How, I thought wildly, had I forgotten to tell my husband and the others the one thing that would have made them believe my story, about the stain on the cupboard wall that could only have been fresh blood? I raced past Honore into the dressing room and examined the place I had touched the night before.

There was no stain now. No trace of one! Had I dreamed the whole thing? But the marks were still on my fingers! I remembered it all so clearly now. Shock and my husband's disbelief, must have temporarily driven the memory of it out of my head until now.

Honore followed me into the dressing room.

"What is it, madame?"

I fought to keep my voice calm as I took a ragged breath. "You said you knew what—

happened here last night?"

"Yes. Miss Samantha told me. It was frightening for you, madame, but—"

"You don't understand," I broke in. "I didn't tell them everything. I forgot, you see, until this moment, when I was wiping my fingers on the napkin."

"I beg your pardon, madame?"

I held out my hand to her. The fingertips were stained a darkish brown.

She glanced down at them for a moment, and then her head came up like a startled horse, her eyes flew wide open and she said one word:

"Blood!"

"Yes," I said. "I saw something wet, glistening on the wall here. I touched the place, and when I put my fingers under the light I saw it was blood. That's when I began screaming."

Her face had gone the same mottled, clamshell color I had seen the night before, and her black eyes were again trancelike and unseeing.

"Honore!" I cried, "what is it, what does it mean? There is no stain on the wall, no sign of one. But if I wet my fingers you will see this is blood. I did not dream it!"

"No," her voice seemed to come from a great distance, and she seemed to force the words out, "you did not dream it, madame. We must talk of this, but not here—not now. Tonight when I help you prepare for bed. I cannot say more now!" She turned from me and poured water for me to wash.

Puzzled, all I could do was accept her abrupt change as I had the first time.

When I wet my fingers and showed them to her, she merely nodded curtly and then went to take my day clothes from the *armoire*. I saw that instinctively she chose the right costume, even the one I would have chosen, and she laid out the proper accessories. She seemed to know a great deal more than any maid I had ever met; certainly she was better educated, but she was an enigma to me. Somehow she didn't fit into this old English manor, no matter how long it had been standing on American southern soil. Yet she had told me her forebears had always served the Rawlins family.

Honore helped me into a green sprigged muslin gown, with three quarter sleeves. She also laid out on the dressing table a wide-brimmed leghorn hat with green ribbons to tie under the chin, a green and white silk parasol, my green silk reticule and white mesh gloves. She had dressed my hair simply in a thick braided coronet with two coral side combs. I chose a single strand of matching coral beads that had been my mother's, and a coral bracelet shaped like a coiled snake. The set had come from China in the days when my grandfather had sailed there.

As I went downstairs, the great house seemed deserted, brooding in its own aged silence. At the foot of the stairs the little maid who had brought my breakfast and was now wielding a duster, told me that the ladies awaited me on the terrace. She led me into another drawing room, all done in delicate faded blues, with French gilt furniture. Through a wall of open French doors, I could see a wide stone terrace. It had a carved balustrade and stone jars brilliant with bougainvillea, and beyond was a formal garden with a maze of privet, badly in need of attention. I heard voices and as I stepped through the doors I found Persis and Aunt Samantha seated in wicker chairs, evidently enjoying some private joke. They looked up startled at my sudden entrance for which I apologized, but Samantha patted a chair next to her and said instantly, "We've been waiting for you, my dear. Come sit down next to me. Did you breakfast well?"

"Yes, I said, "and thank you for sending it to me in bed."

"We don't usually breakfast in bed," she exchanged a smile with Persis, "but I thought, since our disturbance last night"—she colored prettily and added—"do forgive my mentioning it, Tamson. It quite upset dear Breckenridge, he's such an emotional man. But there, we must talk of pleasanter things."

I was thinking that my husband was the coldest, least emotional man I had ever encountered, unless it concerned Harlequin House. Aloud I said, "Honore tells me we are going to Croix this afternoon."

Persis looked sullen and broke out suddenly with, "I don't see why I can't go, too!"

"Now Persis, Breckenridge has already told you that you couldn't. He and Tamson are going on business."

"I could visit while they are doing business."

"Yes, why couldn't she?" I asked.

But Persis, instead of brightening at my suggestion, gave me a black look. What ailed the girl?

Aunt Samantha said primly, "It would not be proper for a young lady to go calling alone, and I'm afraid I'm not feeling too well today."

"Oh, I'm sorry," I said, "is there anything I can do?"

She brightened a bit. "No, my dear, it's my heart. Like my mother I was never too strong, and this heat—it's always been a difficult time of year for Malot and Girole women. But Honore knows what to do for me. I'll just rest here and Persis will keep me company, won't you, child?"

The girl looked furious, and suddenly got up and left us. In a few moments we heard the sound of the piano being played crashingly.

"I'm afraid Persis has the family temper," said her aunt. "A family curse, really. All of them have a touch of it, like the Rawlins. Some of their actions, especially in the old days, were quite disgraceful. My poor mother was upset at the thought of Emilie marrying into the Rawlins family. But Geoffrey, Breckenridge's father, was quite mild really." She touched the corner of her eye with her handkerchief. "And so kind to me when

Mother died. He insisted I come here."

"Then you've been at Harlequin many years, like Honore?"

A subtle change came over her rounded face; she was still a very pretty woman I thought, though faded. She must at one time have been a beauty in that soft clinging way, so pleasing to many men. Perhaps if I had been more that type John Markham would have—but that way only lay despair and loneliness. I put the thought from me forcibly.

"No," she said, "I visited often, but I only came here to live shortly before the war, when the Girole property was sold. A few short years of—heaven. And then it was all ended." Her eyes rose to mine swimming in tears.

"Don't," I said, "please don't, Aunt Samantha. Remember what Breckenridge said." I realized suddenly it was the first time I used my husband's Christian name. "You are to forget the war. In this house we must make a new beginning."

"Yes," she sighed, "yes, that is right. But oh, my dear, if you could have seen this place in the old days!"

"Tell me about it," I said soothingly. "I used to dream about the lovely old plantations, the beautiful belles, the gallant men." It was a lie, but it served to stop her tears.

"Did you, child? That's why Breckenridge must have seemed so romantic to you."

"Of course," I lied again, and then hoping to pique her interest further said, "tell me about Harlequin. As a matter of fact you promised to show me over the house this morning."

"Yes! I'd forgotten all about it. Come, we'll do the lower floor at least, before Breckenridge returns, and I'll tell you all about it as we go along."

I was relieved to see her in better spirits, and followed her into the French drawing room. "It's lovely," I said.

"Yes. Always referred to as the ladies' drawing room." She led me down the main hall to another room and opened the double doors. I was aghast at its size—a huge gleaming expanse of polished floor, a gallery above, and leaded French windows in a bank with doors opening onto another stone terrace with a fountain beyond.

"The grand ballroom, my dear. Oh, the balls I have attended in this place! And nothing of course to what it must have been in the past." Her soft brown eyes dreamed openly. "Just *think* of the personages who have danced there, Tamson! Royalty and their entourages, great diplomats and heads of state, the gentry!"

"Yes," I agreed, "it must have seen a great deal of history in the making."

"Come," she said closing the doors. "Someday we shall entertain again in proper style at Harlequin, in your honor," she added. "And of course, Persis will be married from Harlequin. There's a chapel, you know. You must get Breckenridge to show it to you."

I wondered why it was not possible for her

to show it to me, but said nothing as she led me across the hall to open another door. There was a note of great pride in her voice as she said, "And this is the library."

I entered and was suddenly transfixed. I had come from a family who revered books and learning. In spite of their seafaring interests, my father and his forebears had attended Harvard. I was no great scholar, but I knew how such a person would feel suddenly confronted by the length and breadth of this room with its superb groined ceiling, its walls lined with shelves from floor to ceiling filled with ancient calf-bound volumes. This library, I thought, must be worth a fortune, if the few volumes I recognized were the first editions they appeared to be, yet neither my husband nor any of the other destitute Rawlins had apparently thought of selling any of its contents. There was a short bank of leaded windows, some of them of stained glass, against one wall, with a window seat underneath. In the center of the room were two very long oak reading tables with matching oak chairs, flanking an immense stone foreplace, and in another corner a large carved oak desk and padded armchair.

Aunt Samantha, noting my glance at the latter, said, "That is where Persis does her writing."

"Writing?"

"Yes, dear, since she left school she's been helping Breckenridge compile a Rawlins family history. She works a little each day, on her uncle's orders."

Somehow I could not see the sullen Persis working willingly in this solemn atmosphere.

It was Persis who came in at that moment to tell us that Breckenridge had returned, and that luncheon was served, though she referred to it in the southern manner as dinner. Dinner, as we knew it in the north, was called supper here.

The meal was a heavy one of beef, rice, gravy, biscuits, and boiled ochra. For dessert we had peach cobbler and the inevitable chicory laden coffee.

My husband, as usual, seemed withdrawn and preoccupied during the meal, but directly afterwards ordered the carriage and informed me we must leave for Croix at once.

I went to my room for my hat, parasol, gloves and bag and joined him in the front drive where he quickly helped me into the waiting carriage and ordered Jason to start.

It was pleasant riding under the arched live oaks with their gently swaying festoons of gray-green moss, and the slight breeze that fanned our faces was welcome.

"Croix isn't too far," said my husband. "It lies just north of us. Are you getting along well with Aunt Samantha and Persis?"

"Yes," I said, "though we know little of each other. Your aunt has been very kind."

"And Persis—hasn't?"

"Well, I'm strange to her, and she's only a child."

"Not in her eyes. In this part of the world,

young girls are often married at her age, or before."

"I must seem very old to her then?" I smiled.

"Hardly that. You probably have more in common than you imagine. Try to draw her out. You may find her very—interesting."

He said very little else on our short journey, other than to point out neighboring plantations, and he never once referred to my experience of the night before. I was amazed at the man, so completely bound up in his interest in the plantation, that nothing else seemed to touch him. I could see now how he had calculatingly married me, used me, and yet I believed he fully meant to keep his part of the bargain, and grant me a divorce at the end of the year. I realized of course, that I did not have to remain at Harlequin, and yet from the very first sight of it I had felt a desire, even a need, to unravel its strange mystery. If live people were responsible for what had happened the night before, I wanted to know who they were. If it was some unseen force, I wanted to know that too. Suddenly I asked my husband point blank, "Is Harlequin haunted?"

For an instant a very strange expression crossed his face, and then he said quickly, "Is that something the servants told you?"

"No, but after last night—"

"You had a bad dream!" he said irritably.

"That's not true. I want to know if Harlequin is supposed to have a ghost. Many old houses are said to have. It's nothing to be ashamed of."

"It's all nonsense!" he exclaimed hotly.

"I don't believe you think it is," I said.

"You're like all women—imaginative! Foolishly romantic! My father knew it was all ridiculous, he told the women—"

"Then there must have been some reason for his remarks."

He gave me a level glance. "You're a very discerning young woman, and a determined one. Yes, there were legends—idiotic ones, geared to the Middle Ages. But the house was torn down and moved, and that was the end of it."

"Was it? Couldn't the ghost—or ghosts—have come along, even if it was moved?"

"You surely don't believe in all that spirit nonsense, Tamson? You've too level a head for that. It's what I—admired most in you. The women here in the south are overly romantic; perhaps it's the fault of their menfolk, who have treated them more like indulged children than women. It's not going to be easy for them to change in this new era, but Persis, and the other young ones like her, must be shown how to make the effort. That's why I keep her working in the library. She's got a good mind. Please don't discuss ghosts with her or anyone else at Harlequin."

After that he lapsed into one of his long, sullen silences, and I fell to studying the countryside. It was very lovely, the fields dotted with cottonwoods and oaks, the land lushly green, and for a time we skirted a river that my husband said was the Cannon.

"Up above," he added, "is the plantation of John Calhoun, Fort Hill." There was a note of pride in his voice for the famous Carolina statesman.

Jason turned then to speak over his shoulder.

"We are here, master."

Ahead I could see a church steeple, tall and thin, rising above the green shrouded trees.

6

Croix, when we reached it, proved to be a typical small southern town, with a square of green lawn fronting the two storied Court House, complete with a pair of ancient cannons and a mildewed statue to some Revolutionary hero. There were two churches; the one with the tall spire was the Catholic Church, the other the Methodist. Around the square were the usual shops and stores. I made out a lawyer's shingle, one belonging to a doctor, and a large smithy and livery barn. There were the usual knots of people gathered under the shade trees on the street corners. Dogs, and even pigs and goats, ambled across the main street, and nowhere did I see anyone in a hurry. It was the most characteristic thing about the south, this total lack of the hustle and bustle one always encountered in the north.

Jason stopped the carriage in front of an

old stone building half overgrown with trumpet vines, and I saw with some surprise that it was the Croix Bank.

My husband helped me down and led me inside. It was a small place, with a worn oak railing closing off the two tellers' windows, and two or three clerks' desks. The clerks wore alpaca jackets and seemed to be just sitting idly at their desks rather than working. My husband nodded to one of them, held open the small gate, and ushered me to a door in the rear. He tapped briefly and threw it open and we stepped into a stifling hot inner office with an open window overlooking a small stream and two weeping willow trees.

A small, plump man bounded from behind the mahogany desk and came forward.

"*Mon cher* Breckenridge, and *Madame* Rawlins, is it not? This is indeed a great pleasure!"

My husband introduced us, telling me that this was Pierre Legros, president of the bank, as his father and grandfather had been before him. Croix had been settled and named by the French, he explained.

Legros, with dark curling hair, a small pointed beard, and merry dark eyes, clicked his heels and bent to kiss my hand in the Continental manner. He handed me into the most comfortable chair with another gallant little bow, motioned my husband to a seat, and returned to his own place behind his desk.

"How is Harlequin, my dear Breckenridge? And your Aunt Samantha?"

"Well, thank you, Pierre. But I fear we haven't time for a proper visit. I wrote you concerning my wishes? If we could proceed with business I would appreciate it."

"Certainly. You wish to open the new account in both names, your wife's and your own?"

"Yes. When I am away Mrs. Rawlins will be in charge at Harlequin, and it is my wish that she be able to withdraw funds for the plantation as needed."

"I understand. You have the funds ready to deposit?"

My husband handed him a thick packet sealed with red wax bearing the seal of the signet ring he wore on his finger.

Legros slit the paper and seals with an ornate paper knife, examined the contents, and a moment later left us to reappear almost at once followed by one of his clerks who handed us several papers to sign.

When everything had been arranged, and my husband had pocketed the deposit book, Legros insisted that we accept at least a glass of sherry. He also issued a warm invitation to dine at his home, but my husband declined claiming that we still had too much business to attend to.

Next Jason drove us up the street to the weathered clapboard building where I had noticed the lawyer's shingle.

In his small shabby office, of which he seemed to be the only occupant other than a colored boy who was sorting some papers in the corner, Virgil Jessup also rose from his desk to greet us. But it was not at all the same type of greeting the dapper little Frenchman had given us.

Jessup was a very tall, rawboned man, probably about the same age as my husband, with a long freckled face and reddish hair, which he wore long with accompanying sideburns. He had light, intelligent eyes, and the ugliest, widest mouth I had ever seen, but displaying the most infectious grin.

"Well, Breck, so this is what's been keepin' you away from Croix?" He put a big hand on my husband's shoulder, and he was the first one I had heard address him as Breck. They were obviously on intimate terms, for my husband was smiling. He introduced us, and Jessup's enormous hand seemed to swallow mine as he shook hands with me. I saw he wore a rumpled white shirt and white linen suit, and his cravat was askew. Behind him there was a very battered straw hat hanging from the knob of his desk chair.

He tossed the hat nonchalantly to the floor, brought the chair forward for me, dusting it off with his soiled handkerchief, and kicked forward two stools for my husband and himself.

"Ma'am," he drawled, "you're a sight for sore eyes in those pretty clothes. Our ladies haven't seen any fashionable new clothes here since—I don't know when. You'll be the talk of Croix." He turned to Mr. Rawlins.

"Did you get my letter, Virgil?" asked my husband.

"Sure, did, boy. Got everythin' just like you wanted, all drawn up an' ready to sign. Quite a little fortune you got; must say I'm glad for Harlequin. Lovely place, an' historic, hate to see it go to ruin. You'll be doin' a lot more for the countryside than gladden our eyesight personally ma'am," he said to me.

I felt uncomfortable under his candid gaze, but was sure that he meant no unkindness to me. I was a northerner, and a rich one, so it would be only natural if these southern people disliked and resented me on sight. My very speech and dress must be an affront to them, but so far I had not encountered any outright hostility. I could read none in Virgil Jessup's eyes.

As he had done in Legros' office, my husband insisted on getting directly to the business at hand.

Reluctantly, I felt, Mr. Jessup complied. He pawed through a drawer in his desk and came up with a will form which I could see had been filled out in a hasty scrawling hand.

"There," he said, "you sign here, Breck. I'll step next door and get the Biggses to witness."

I remembered there was a small mercantile store next door in the same building. He returned in a moment with an elderly sallow man in shirtsleeves, and a very fat woman in a white dress and black sateen apron.

"Mr. an' Miz Biggs," said the lawyer. The

couple nodded but did not speak. I had the impression that they often performed this service for Mr. Jessup. When they had witnessed my husband's signature and that of Jessup, and added their own, they left as quickly and silently as they had come. But I saw Mr. Jessup press something into the man's hand before he left.

"Now," said Jessup, "you want me to file a copy in my safe and give you one, or keep 'em both here?"

"I'll keep one at Harlequin, and you file the other one, Virgil."

"Sure. Now, how about supper up at the Carriage Inn? They cooked a big ham today."

I noted with surprise that it had grown dusk as we completed our business. The day had passed very swiftly.

My husband glanced at me. "Would you like that, my dear?"

"I think it would be very nice." I said it more not to disappoint Mr. Jessup's eager glance, than for my own sake.

"Then we accept, Virgil, but only if you will be our guest."

Jessup seemed both pleased and relieved, for he did not argue the point, but scooped up his sorry looking hat from the floor and held it in his hand as he bowed us over the threshold. He called back over his shoulder to the boy to shut up the office until he returned. The boy mumbled something that I took to be assent, and we walked up the dusty street to the Inn.

The Carriage Inn must have been just that in the old days, but it seemed more taproom and restaurant now, than hotel. The dining room on the ground floor was large, filled with white covered tables, and there was a brick fireplace at one end with a few sagging leather chairs in front of it. The floors felt spongy and the room had a dead, musty odor.

A neat waitress took our order for the baked ham dinner, but another girl brought and served it.

The food was good, but far too heavy for me. There were mustard greens and white grits, covered with red ham gravy, and for dessert some sort of bread pudding with a sticky brown sauce which I barely touched. I was grateful for the tall glass of iced tea, for the damp heat was as oppressive as a wet sheet thrown over my head.

The room was well filled with diners, more men than women, and there were no children present. For the most part the men appeared to be planters, business men and farmers, not as smart as the people I had seen in Charleston. But I enjoyed listening to their soft drawling voices and easy laughter. I kept silent for the most part, not wanting to call attention to my northern accent, though if I had given it any thought I would have realized that by now everyone in Croix must know who I was. But no one seemed to stare at me or watch me covertly, and I contented myself with listening to the conversation between my husband and Virgil Jessup.

The latter was just mopping up the last of his red gravy with a piece of biscuit, and my husband, who had eaten sparingly, was finishing his black coffee. They had been speaking of horses.

"I'm considering going to Kentucky," said my husband. "They are sure to have the best mares."

"Without doubt," agreed the lawyer, "but at the best price, too. You might ask Valerian; he's just back from there. Bought a few head and won a handsome stud at poker."

Something moved across my husband's face, some shadow that was quickly gone, but I realized Jessup had seen it too.

"Look, Breck," he said quietly, "I know there's been some bad blood between you and Clive Valerian in the past, but it's a long time ago, with a war between. You'd both do well to let bygones be bygones. Southerners, beggin' your pardon, ma'am, have got to learn to stick together. Marchmount's nearly in ruins, and the only thing Clive's interested in doing is starting the stables again. His mother and brother Seton are near crazy tryin' to hold the plantation together. Most of their servants have left, though where the poor devils have gone I don't know. The roads are full of 'em begging for a meal or a roof."

"Valerian should have kept his people and offered them work for shares," said my husband. "That's what I did. At least they didn't starve, and now thank God, I can start paying wages. I sympathize with Mrs. Valerian and Seton, but I have no patience with men like Valerian, who refuse to change with the times, come hell or high water."

"That's exactly right," said a tight voice behind us.

I turned as did the others to see a tall, high shouldered figure, dressed quite elegantly in gray, with a cream figured waistcoat, holding a beaver hat in one hand. He was the age of my husband and Mr. Jessup, I judged, but with harsh lines in his wide-cheeked face and around his deep set yellowish eyes that gave him an older, more dissolute appearance. His chin was long, and the mouth below his silky fair moustache was wire thin and cynical. His hair was also fair, almost white, and I realized with something of a shock that he was the first man I had ever met whom I instantly mistrusted. There was nothing outwardly sinister about him, save his mouth perhaps, but there was the inherent coldness in him that one senses at sight of a snake.

I sensed that he would have no compuction about destroying anything that got in his way or thwarted his desires. He was a man who looked as if he had never cared, or had ceased to care, about anything save his own whims and vices. For this reason I realized the danger in him, under the languidly smiling exterior, and I could see my husband felt much as I did. He rose to his feet, however, as did Mr. Jessup who was saying nervously:

"Mrs. Rawlins, may I present an old friend and neighbor, Mr. Clive Valerian, of Marchmount. Clive, Mrs. Rawlins."

Clive Valerian bent over my hand with practiced grace.

"Your servant, madame."

Our glance met briefly and I disliked the dancing devilish light that glowed for an instant in his yellowish eyes. They were like the eyes of a tiger, unwinking and savage. He bowed briefly to my husband, saying, "I've heard of the good fortune of Harlequin, and may I add my congratulations on your own behalf."

My husband murmured something through tight lips, and then noticing every eye in the room on us, said quickly, "Won't you join us, Valerian?"

"Thank you." He sat down gracefully between Mr. Jessup and me, and Virgil Jessup stepped at once into the breach.

"Clive, Breck here, has been thinkin' of going to Kentucky after some breedin' stock. I told him you're just back from there on the same business."

"Goin' to start up your stable again?" Valerian asked in his insolent drawl.

"Yes."

"You'll find the hosses'll come dear. Cost me a packet for four mares an' a filly."

When the waitress came he ordered a Planter's Punch, but refused food.

My husband seemed to have gotten himself under control again. He said quite civilly, "I heard you've got a good stud."

Valerian laughed, "That was a piece of

damned fine luck, beggin' pardon ma'am. Won him in a poker game from Colonel Fulham. An Arab, with Darley blood."

I saw my husband's eye brighten with interest. "Has Fulham got much of a stable?"

"Hell no, all gone to pot. Only thing he had was this stud, three mares an' a damned fine little filly. But he wouldn't sell one of 'em."

"Then how did you get him to part with the stud?"

Valerian's cat's eyes gleamed. "Old boy thought he'd do me in the eye and enrich his own stables. There was a helluva pot on the table, plus two of my mares, an' he couldn't resist it."

"And," said my husband coldly, "he was probably drunk."

Valerian's face grew taut and ugly. "Damn you, Rawlins, take care—even if your rich Northern lady wife is present."

Breckenridge swore under his breath and both men jumped to their feet. Once more we were the target for every eye in the place. Virgil Jessup stood up between them, a big hand on the shoulder of each.

"Gentlemen, please! There are ladies present, and this is no proper place for—differences."

"You're right, Virgil," said Clive Valerian softly, "my humble apologies, ma'am." To my husband he added, "Another time, another place, Rawlins."

He turned and left us. I had not known until that moment that he wore silver spurs on the heels of his boots, and the sound of them as he stalked away seemed to issue a note of warning. I felt a shiver of apprehension run up my spine.

Mr. Jessup saw us to our carriage, but we did not catch another glimpse of Mr. Valerian, and I was relieved when we were headed back for Harlequin.

"I'm sorry about what happened," my husband said presently, "Valerian and I have never seen—eye to eye."

"I understand," I said, but I wished he had told me what lay behind their deep dislike for one another. Perhaps, I thought, Honore would know. More and more I realized how much I was coming to depend on her. Because I was feeling a bit guilty about counting more upon her than upon my husband, I asked, "When will you be leaving on your trip?"

"Next week if possible. That will be the first of the month. I should return in a few weeks. You won't mind running the place that long?"

"No," I said, "I'll do my best."

He put his hand briefly over mine. "I know you will, Tamson, and I'll be most grateful. You deserve a great deal more than you're getting here. I hope that in the future you will find everything that you have ever wanted." He added more slowly, "Do you feel very badly still about John Markham and Lucy?"

A sharp pang shot through my heart, but I wouldn't let him see how I really felt. "No," I forced myself to say, "I want them both to be happy. There's so little real happiness in the world."

"You're a generous person, little Tamson. John Markham is a fool."

I colored and glanced out the window.

He said hastily, "We haven't had much chance to fix the place up, but if you like we'll give a party before I leave. Would you like that? It would please Aunt Samantha and Persis."

I did not really feel in the mood for a party, for mention of John had made me sad. I said, "Why don't we wait until your return? Meanwhile Aunt Samantha and Persis and I can get the whole place in order and ready for it, and the women will have time to get a new wardrobe made."

He smiled. "Your thoughtfulness again. I'm afraid I don't know all the things that please women. Yes, of course that would be better. A grand ball, then, in the old tradition of Harlequin? There hasn't been one since before the war. Spend whatever you have to, but it must be the money from the bank you use, do you understand?" He gave me the pass book. "Someday I will be paying all this back to you, because Harlequin will make its way again on its own. I promise you that."

"I'm sure of it," I said, and we rode home in a more companionable silence than we had yet known. It was only his sudden question about John that had given me an unhappy moment. It all seemed to have happened such a long time ago now, yet I knew that for the rest of my life any thought of John, my first love, was bound to bring me heartache. And I wondered what my life would be like when I left Harlequin.

It was quite late when we got back and my husband asked again if I wanted to move from my bedroom to other quarters.

"I don't want you to go through again what you did last night," he said.

"I'm really not afraid," I replied. "Honore will be there until I go to sleep, I'm sure, and after all I did sleep there last night and am none the worse for it."

"As you wish," he said. Then he excused himself to go to his study, and I went up to my room. Persis and Aunt Samantha had retired already, it seemed.

Honore rose from an armchair where she had been doing some sewing while she waited for me.

"Did madame have a nice trip?" she asked.

"Very nice, thank you, Honore, but I'm rather tired."

"Of course, madame. I will help you get ready for bed."

She did so with her usual deft movements. I saw she had already laid out my night clothes. When I was ready she took down my hair to brush and braid it. Our eyes met in the spotted glass and I said, "Honore, you promised to talk to me tonight—about what happened."

"That is so, madame."

"I know it wasn't just a dream, or a figment of my imagination. And you agreed."

"Yes, madame. But I must ask first what the master said about it."

"He refused to discuss it, really," I said. "He dismissed it as imagination or hallucination. I even asked him if the house was—haunted."

"Did you, madame?"

"He just said there had been legends since the Middle Ages, but that both he and his father disbelieved the tales."

She said nothing, putting away my brush and comb.

"Honore, for heaven's sake, tell me, is Harlequin House haunted?"

"Yes, madame, of course it is haunted."

"By what?" I asked. "By whom? Tell me the legends if you know them."

She stood with her back to the cupboard wall, arms folded across her bosom. She had a strange, almost aristocatic face. There was pride there and intelligence and something I could not quite fathom.

"I told you, madame, my family had long served the Rawlinses?"

I nodded.

"My forebears were Nubians. During the First Crusade, when Lord Caton Rawlins—the family had been called Roi Launs in Normandy before the Conquest—went to the Holy Lands, he returned with my ancestor, Alir, as his arms bearer. Alir had been the prize slave of a Moor whom Caton had slain. But

Lord Caton set him free, and took him back to England, because Alir asked to go. He remained all his life in the Rawlins household, and his family after him, because he chose to have it so.

"Alir took a French sewing maid as his bride. Her family name was Delacroix, and since he had no last name, he adopted it. So we have remained Delacroix. His descendants were present when Harlequin House was built. His male descendants served the Rawlins men, and the females, the women of the household. Both were given the advantages of education and books.

"The legends you ask about began when Harlequin was new. A young girl of high birth, a ward of King Henry VII, was to marry the then young Lord William Rawlins. She did not do so happily. She loved a member of the King's Guard. These were her rooms, the bridal suite, though there was not at that time a connecting door between the apartments of husband and wife, but merely a short hall. She had her maid cover it with broken glass, knowing her husband would come that way barefooted.

"After the wedding ceremony and celebration, she retired early to this apartment with her maids. One was a Delacroix, and she discovered the glass. While the bride was being readied for bed, she secretly swept it up and told her master, Lord William.

"When the bride was alone, she admitted her lover from the closet here." She pointed to the door behind her with the sprung frame. "As he came out and into her arms, William Rawlins, standing in the passage, hurled a knife at him. It caught him in the throat, pinning him to the door. They say the blood-stain remained for many years despite every effort to remove it."

I was suddenly cold and horrified. "And the bride?"

"She was his wife, madame. William spent the night with her, but in the morning she threw herself out of the bedroom window. She broke her neck. Ever since, the sound of her walking in the dressing room as she awaits her lover, is heard by the brides of Harlequin House."

"And—the blood last night?" I was aghast at her tale, and the mute walls surrounding me that had witnessed that horrible crime of long ago.

Honore's eyes widened and darkened. "Ah, *that* has been seen by very few brides, madame."

"And what does it mean?"

"A grave danger, I am afraid, madame. Always—danger."

"Danger of what? To whom?"

"To either you or your husband, madame."

My old Puritan upbringing suddenly rebelled. "I don't believe it," I said stoutly, "not one word of it!"

"You saw the blood, madame. Only a few have seen that—it always spells *danger!*"

"I saw some blood, but someone could have put it there, or it could have been animal blood."

Her eyes opened very wide. "Madame, you refuse to believe what I have told you? But that is even more dangerous, for then you will not be on your guard!"

"Honore," I said gently, "I think that you believe what you have told me, and perhaps others do, too. But I know my husband doesn't believe it, and while the legends may have some basis for truth, I am sure the ghosts have none. If anyone in this house is hoping to frighten me by all this, it's no use. I simply don't believe it—and I'm not afraid."

Honore made a strange sign with her hand, and said, "Madame, I have tried to serve you, warn you, but you will not listen. You do not understand. These spirits in the house, they are determined and ugly; they seek only to destroy the Rawlinses."

It was on the tip of my tongue to tell her that I was not a real Rawlins, nor would I ever be, but something kept me from it. The ghosts hadn't harmed me on the previous night and I was not afraid of them now.

"Thank you, Honore," I said, "but I am tired now."

In silence she helped me into bed, tucked the net about me and left. In spite of her frightful tales, I fell asleep at once, and it was broad daylight when I awakened.

7

My husband left a week later, and although a complete stranger to the household and the plantation, I found myself in charge of both.

I saw at once that Persis resented my authority most deeply, but I tried to ignore it. After all, she was young and spoiled, and in many ways I felt, thwarted. Aunt Samantha on the other hand, was most cooperative. She took me on a complete tour of the house and showed me where everything was. Even though so many rooms had been closed off for years, there was still an enormous amount of living space still in use. Like many old manors, Harlequin had miles of what seemed to me useless corridors, nooks, and crannies, and I realized it would be easy to get lost in such a vast place.

In time, I managed to evolve a routine that suited me, and seemed to keep things moving smoothly. In the mornings, after an early breakfast, I went to my husband's office-study, where Honore joined me to go over daily household requirements. We never mentioned our last talk in the dressing room of my suite, and I determined that we never should.

When Honore had gone, I would enter, in a personal record I was keeping, what supplies had been issued and what decisions had been made. I wanted to be able to put the record before my husband when he returned. When I had finished, I sent for Forbes. I still did not particularly like him, but I knew for the sake of the plantation I must put aside my personal feelings so that we could work together.

I told him that I did not care to ride a horse on our rounds of inspection, so he brought around a light surrey and drove me over the plantation.

I had not dreamed, in spite of Harlequin's now reduced circumstances, that it would be so large or that there would be so much work involved. Workers seemed to be everywhere in the fields, hoeing cotton, working in the corn and bean patches, or tending the rice that grew in the rust colored paddies, with brilliant darting redbirds flashing through the veils of gray moss overhead. It was a lush, somnolent countryside, and I could see how one could fall under its strange, overpowering spell. There was none of the crisp brilliance of the north, but instead a nostalgic haunting beauty that overcame one by degrees.

Along the way, Forbes, who really did seem to know his business, pointed out places of interest, and showed me crops that needed attention, fences that had to be repaired, outbuildings that required new roofing, and animals that would be butchered or sold. I was surprised at the diversity of the farming on Harlequin. I had always thought somehow that a plantation was a more or less one crop institution, raising either tobacco, cotton or indigo. But I found that while any or all of these staple crops might be grown, a great many more things were required to run a plantation.

There were sizeable vegetable gardens, a fruit orchard, grain for the livestock, a poultry yard, milk cows, and a good number of hogs.

Even though I was ignorant of most of the farm terms Forbes mentioned, I hoped that I gave the impression that *I* was making the decisions.

"You seem to know a great deal about farming," I told him as we jogged along.

"Yes, ma'am, I was raised hereabouts."

"On Harlequin?"

He shook his tow colored head, his blue eyes bright between white lashes. "Over Charleston way. My Pa was old Jules Girole's overseer."

"Then you've known the family for a long time?"

"Yes, ma'am. The Girole plantation was lost durin' the war, and after I got out of the army, Mr. Rawlins gave me a job here."

I said nothing more, for I could sense a bitterness in him. The war, I thought, had left hurt and resentment everywhere, and it seemed it would exist for a long time to come. I was glad in a way, that my northern money would be used to rebuild this great old plantation to what it had once been.

When we arrived back at the house, I was surprised to see a magnificent chestnut stallion tethered to the iron hitching post in front. I saw Forbes give the animal an appraising glance as he helped me down from the surrey.

"Do you know whose horse that is?" I asked, but he merely shook his head.

Honore opened the door for me, and when I asked who our visitor was, she said it was Mr. Seton Valerian, calling upon Miss Persis. I nodded and went to my room to freshen up. When I came downstairs I found Aunt Samantha, Persis, and a young man dressed in riding clothes, waiting for me in the drawing room.

Persis, I noted, had a look of defiance on her young face, while Aunt Samantha, for some reason, seemed nervous and afraid.

"Tamson, my dear," she began at once as if in a rush to get the words out, "this young gentleman is a friend of the family's from Croix. Mr. Seton Valerian, of Marchmount. Seton, Mrs. Rawlins."

The young man bowed, came forward with a boyish smile, and took my hand. I could see nothing of his brother, Clive, in him. For one thing he was so much younger than the obnoxious Clive, that they must have had little in common growing up. Seton looked hardly more than a boy. He was not overly tall, but was slender and muscular like a picture I had seen of a bullfighter, with the same keen, striking good looks. His hands were graceful but strong looking. I could imagine him having little trouble controlling the fleet looking horse I had seen in front. His smile, a white flash in his thin face, was appealing and gay.

"I hope I'm not intrudin', Mrs. Rawlins," he drawled. "I was just ridin' by on my way back from Charleston, and thought I might pay my respects to Miss—to the family, ma'am."

Persis said sharply, "We've invited him to take dinner with us."

"Of course," I said, ignoring the spite of Persis' tone. "I believe it's ready and waiting. Will you escort Aunt Samantha in, Mr. Valerian?"

"My pleasure, ma'am."

Persis and I followed them into the dining room where fans moved slowly above the table, pulled by two young Negro boys.

I was glad Honore and I had chosen a suitable menu for the hot day. We had chilled melon balls, a delicate sole cooked in the French manner with shaved almonds, creamed chicken on biscuit, and cherry tarts.

Seton and I tried to keep the conversation going, with some help from Aunt Samantha, but Persis was quite deliberate in her sultry silence. I felt very annoyed with her, especially since the young man had obviously come to call upon her.

"You may not be aware," I told Seton, "but I met your brother in Croix, a short time ago."

If I had suddenly slapped all three of them across the face I could not have produced more shock and consternation there.

"Clive?" murmured Persis and Aunt Samantha together, and I saw their startled glances lock for an instant.

Seton had flushed and lowered his eyes, his fingers crumbling the bread on his plate with deliberate violence.

"Yes, Mr. Clive Valerian—he *is* your brother isn't he?" I asked Seton.

"Yes ma'am," admitted the young man, but his voice had a strangled sound.

Aunt Samantha's hands fluttered as she endeavored to bridge the trying moment. "It's only surprising to us, Tamson dear, because one so seldom sees Clive in town these days. And—you will pardon my mentioning it, Seton—Breckenridge and Clive had a disagreement in the past."

Seton raised his head. There was still a hot color over his cheekbones, but his jaw was determined. "My brother and Breckenridge Rawlins fought a duel many years ago. They haven't spoken often since. That is the whole story, Mrs. Rawlins."

"I—see." I felt that this was a personal matter between the two families, and I had no right to pry further into it. Perhaps, I thought, my husband would tell me about it himself someday, or Honore would explain it to me. In any case I had no wish to prolong the tension and misery I felt at the table. I deliberately changed the subject. "That is a very handsome horse you have in front," I told Seton.

His relief at my words was almost pathetic. "He really is a beauty, isn't he? The most wonderful withers and cannon bone I've ever seen. He has intelligence, too. You could teach him anything. Of course he's green yet, only just been broken to the saddle, but he learns fast. He's not mine though." He said the last with a note of regret.

"That's a pity," I said. "Who does own him?"

"Clive—my brother. He—he won him in Kentucky. He lets me ride him, because I've been training the horses at Marchmount. I understand your husband plans to restock the stables here at Harlequin?"

"He hopes to reclaim everything on the plantation," I said.

"With his rich wife's dowry," said Persis in a taut angry voice.

"Persis!" Aunt Samantha half rose in her chair. "How dare you speak to Breckenridge's wife like that! Apologize at once, miss!"

Persis' chin was high, her cheeks white with fury.

"It's the truth," she said. "Everyone knows it!"

"Of course it's true," I said calmly. "If your cousin has married a rich woman, and his property—which is also hers now, is in need of repairs, isn't it only sensible that he use that money to rebuild their home? I am going to live here, I want very much to see Harlequin restored."

But my cool acceptance of her words only seemed to infuriate her more. Persis jumped to her feet overturning her chair. "You *bought* Cousin Breckenridge, and this plantation and Harlequin House, with your Yankee money! I hate every cent of it—and I hate you!" Raging tears welled up suddenly in her green eyes, and she raced from the room.

Seton looked thunderstruck, and Aunt Samantha was wringing her hands and whimpering like a wounded animal.

"Oh my, oh my, what must you think of us? How can I ask you to forgive her? Persis is still a child, I'm afraid. She doesn't really understand anything. Dear Tamson, do try to overlook this hysterical outburst. I'm sure when she reconsiders you'll find she didn't mean a word she said. Oh, if Breckenridge were only here!"

"Please don't distress yourself," I said kindly. "I suppose my coming here has been very hard on Persis. And she has been through a lot in her young life."

"Oh, no, it isn't that," wailed Aunt Samantha, "I truly don't know what's come over the girl!"

"It's all right, Aunt Samantha, I understand. Please don't say anymore."

Aunt Samantha dabbed at her eyes and nose. "You're very kind, Tamson, much kinder than that naughty child deserves! I'll go up and speak to her."

"Perhaps it would be better to leave her alone for now."

"Do you think so? Well, perhaps you are right. This whole thing has unsettled my nerves. I must go and lie down for a while. I'll get Honore to mix me a draught."

"Yes, that would be best," I told her soothingly. "And please don't worry. I'll talk to Persis later."

"Bless you, my dear." Aunt Samantha made a hasty retreat, after bidding Seton a distracted goodbye and asking to be remembered to his mother.

Seton and I wandered out to the terrace and down into the overgrown garden. I found that after the double embarrassment of my mention of his brother, Clive, and Persis' outburst against me, Seton seemed to have recovered his boyish high spirits. He was really a very attractive young man, and I thought that Persis must find him so, too. Perhaps this had helped bring on her tirade against me; maybe she resented having to share anything else with me, especially if she felt my wealth was something she could never hope to compete with. She couldn't possibly dream, of course, how empty all her fears were. I was merely a sojourner at Harlequin.

"Tell me about Marchmount," I said to Seton presently as we walked. At once his youthful face lighted up, as it had at mention of the horse.

"It used to be one of the grand old

estates, like Harlequin, in my father's and grandfather's time. The stables and racetrack were famous, just as they were here. The house isn't as old, of course. It was built by my great-grandfather for his bride in Colonial times. Then, of course, all the countryside around Croix and outside Charleston for that matter, was mainly unsettled territory. You must come to visit my mother," he added rather shyly. "She doesn't see many people, and since the war"—he paused, looking confused, as so many Southerns seemed to do in my presence.

"The war was terrible for both sides," I said firmly, "but it *is* over. My husband has a rule in this house: we are to mention the subject in the future."

He looked relieved. "That is a very good rule, ma'am. I just wish—others would observe it too."

"Your brother," I asked, "does he speak often of the war?"

"He hardly talks of anything else. He is still very bitter. He lost a great deal in the war, not more than some others I guess, but he feels it more keenly. The Valerians were always looked up to, a power in South Carolina. At one time he had political ambitions, and he did serve with Jeff Davis, but now of course all that is lost. He can't seem to settle down to plantation life anymore. If he could, I think he would sell out and move to England or the West Indies. He—he's lost interest in Marchmount."

"But you haven't?"

He looked startled as if I had touched on a hidden recess in his mind. "No. I don't suppose I ever will. It's like this place to me." He glanced up at the great building behind us. "There's so much of history, of what has gone before, here. And if it's your home you owe an allegiance to it. You want to add to its lustre, not walk off and leave it. It's a trust you hope to pass on to your own children."

"You and your brother are very different."

He glanced down at the path. "I suppose we are. But then I haven't seen as much of the world as Clive has, or been through what he has. I was very young during the war years."

I smiled at him. "Your mother must have been very glad of that?"

He returned my smile. "I reckon so." He pulled a large hunter watch out of his waist-coat pocket and flipped back the lid. "I must be goin', ma'am. I thank you for dinner, and I hope you'll convey my best wishes to Miss Samantha and Miss Persis?"

"Of course. And I'll walk out with you and see this lovely animal of yours."

His face shone with pleasure. "Thank you, ma'am."

In the drive I stood watching as he tightened his saddle girth, picked up the reins and vaulted lightly into the saddle. The stallion, his hide glistening like polished mahogany, rose up on his hind feet and for an instant I was afraid he was going over backwards. But Seton spoke softly to him and reined him expertly around, then in a flash it seemed they were disappearing down the tree-lined drive.

A voice behind me said, "That's sure a likely lookin' stud Valerian's got himself."

I turned to find Forbes standing with his straw hat in his hand, watching the disappearing horse and rider with avid interest. I hadn't heard him come up behind me and I was annoyed.

Forbes seemed unaware of my displeasure, or else chose to deliberately ignore it. I had the fleeting impression that though he disliked me, he was making skillful use of me somehow for his own purposes. But that was ridiculous. How could he? And why should he even attempt such a thing? I was growing suspicious of everyone.

I deliberately eased the lines of my face and said conversationally, "I hope Mr. Rawlins will return with one just as fine."

"But he won't, ma'am, not one like that."

"Why not?" I asked, nettled. "He has plenty of money to buy whatever animals he wants."

That, I saw, had touched Forbes on the raw. Something hard and ugly came into his china blue eyes. "There are some things can't be bought, ma'am. Horseflesh like that is one of 'em. No Kentucky breeder would part with a stallion like that—not willingly. He was a win, that's what."

"What do you mean?"

"Mr. Clive Valerian won him in a poker

game, I heard tell. Only way he could've got him."

I remembered then that Clive Valerian had told us as much.

"Well," I said stubbornly, wanting to wipe off the smirk on the overseer's face. "If Mr. Rawlins really wants such a horse, I'm sure he can get him."

This remark only seemed to increase Forbes' truculence. "You're dead wrong, ma'am, if you think Mr. Clive would ever sell Mr. Rawlins anythin' from Marchmount, no sir!"

"You seem very sure of that," I said, feeling less sure of my ground every minute, and growing angry because of it.

"Some things such as death an' taxes, ma'am. Valerians an' Rawlins don't cotton to each other, not one little bit."

"That's nonsense," I said hotly. "Mr. Seton Valerian was our luncheon guest. You saw him!"

He laughed, one short harsh sound that grated on my ears.

"That young gent came just for one reason—to flaunt that stud in the eyes of Harlequin, ma'am."

"You are quite mistaken," I said, using all the disdain I could muster. "He came to issue an invitation to me to call at Marchmount—tomorrow." I added the last in reckless defiance, and was appalled the next moment. How could I carry it off?"

But my words produced the desired

result. Forbes' jaw went slack and his eyes mirrored reluctant belief.

"Tomorrow?"

"Exactly," I lied crisply. "Miss Persis and I will be going in the morning. Please instruct Jason to bring around the carriage at nine o'clock sharp."

I turned on my heel and marched confidently into the house, barely aware of his awed, "Yes, Mrs. Rawlins," behind me.

8

The next morning, a humid but beautiful one without a cloud in the serene cobalt blue sky, Persis and I were on our way to March-mount, and I still hadn't the slightest idea of what I intended saying to the Valerians when we got there. Just as the night before, I had had no idea of how I could approach Persis to suggest that she accompany me.

In the end I had simply gone to her room, for she had not come down to the supper table, and I had found her lying on her four poster bed with her hands behind her fair head and a sullen look on her pretty young face.

She greeted me with, "I suppose you've come for an apology? Aunt Samantha says I owe you one. I suppose I do, as a lady, but I don't feel like a lady right now."

"Being a lady is difficult," I said. "Many times when I've had to act like one, I've not felt in the least ladylike."

She gave me a quick glance. I had seated myself in a chair near the bed. The room was large and airy, but with threadbare drapes, rugs and upholstery, as in the rest of the house.

I said lightly, "I know you think I have bought my way here. Harlequin has great antiquity and history behind it. But you must understand that I knew nothing of the plantation or Harlequin House—not even its name, when I married your cousin."

She looked at me fully now in astonishment. "You knew nothing of—Harlequin?"

"No. My husband never mentioned his family or his property when we were married, except to say that someday he hoped to restore his lands."

Persis sat straight up in bed, her green eyes questioning me, "He married you—for love?"

I lied again, because I thought I had to under the circumstances. "Yes. Is it so strange?"

"No"—it was barely a whisper—"I only thought—"

"Yes?" I prompted.

She shook her head, and the stubborn look came back to her jaw. "It doesn't matter now." She turned to me quickly. "I—I guess I didn't really understand. Cousin Breckenridge is sometimes very strange, and I suppose that's why your two rooms—well, why he acted so funny the night you had the nightmare. I apologize Cousin Tamson."

I didn't trust her complete about-face, but I said, "Thank you, Persis. And since we now understand each other, would you do me a favor?"

Her eyes grew cautious, but she said, "Of course, Cousin Tamson."

"Would you go to Croix with me tomorrow—to visit Marchmount?"

She stiffened, and seemed about to refuse, and then saw my eyes regarding her levelly and she said, "Yes, of course, if you wish it." But there was no joy in her tone to see Seton again, as I had thought there would be.

And so we were on our way in the sunlight, the green and brown landscape fleeting before us, and I wondered what the outcome of my foolish passage at arms with Forbes would be when we reached Marchmount.

I wondered if Clive Valerian would be there, and how he would receive us if he were. I was suddenly frightened, for Clive Valerian had seemed a violent man, and I sensed he did not like me. I might be leading Persis into an ugly situation that my husband would certainly disapprove of. I glanced at Jason in the driver's seat, but I knew he could give us little support. Still, there was Mrs. Valerian. Surely calling upon her, at Seton's suggestion, could not be taken amiss? In view of the family situation between the Rawlinses and Valerians—and from what I had seen in the faces of Clive Valerian and my husband when they met at the Inn—I did not doubt that a deep animosity existed between them. Nevertheless, I was determined to carry through our visit to Marchmount, no matter what the consequences.

Marchmount lay about five miles from Croix, fronted by a small stream no doubt that flowed in back of the bank at Croix. The drive leading to the house was rutted and dusty, but well shaded by willows and cottonwoods, and I could see a few field hands working unsuperintended, in a desultory way, in the fields beyond.

From a distance, the white Colonial house with its Corinthian columns and wide verandas, appeared large and gracious. It was only after we had stopped in front that I saw the sign of decay and neglect. The white paint was chipped and peeling, and window frames were warped. One green shutter, lacking a hinge, hung like a broken bird's wing, and the cane furniture on the veranda had a sagging, forlorn look.

Jason helped us down and stood hat in hand while we mounted the steps. The front door was standing open and I could see into the cool, dim hall. I rapped on the door, and after what seemed a long time, an aged colored maid in turban and felt slippers, came forward to meet us.

"We are calling upon Mrs. Valerian," I said crisply. "Tell her it is Mrs. Breckenridge

Rawlins and Miss Persis Girole."

The old woman showed no surprise, but just stood blinking at us in the sunlight.

I thought perhaps she had not heard, and started to repeat myself, when I became aware of footsteps coming up the porch stairs behind us. I turned to find Seton standing there regarding us with surprise and a trace of consternation. He masked both emotions quickly and said warmly, "Mrs. Rawlins, Miss Persis, this is very nice. Cleta, go tell my mother the ladies are here." To us he said, "Won't you come in?"

He ushered us inside and down the spacious hall into a charming but now woefully shabby drawing room. I noticed that Seton wore the same riding clothes he had worn at Harlequin the day before. Perhaps he had no others.

He made polite conversation until his mother joined us a few minutes later.

If there was ill feeling between the Valerians and the Rawlinses, Mrs. Valerian, when she greeted us, showed only delighted surprise and a cordial warmth. She was a thin, weary looking woman, with something of the same faded, neglected grandeur of her house. She must have once been a great beauty, I thought, but care or illness or both had worn deep lines in her pale face, as rock is eroded by constant rain weeping against it.

She sent Cleta for iced drinks and some delicious little spice cakes, and told us that we must stay for dinner, for her eldest son would be home then. She said the words uncertainly in her rather high voice, and Seton at once changed the subject.

"I've been working with Hamid this morning," he said, "the stud I rode to Harlequin."

This exactly suited my purpose and I said, "May we see him, and the other horses of course? I know so little about horses; that is one reason I came. If we are to build up the stables at Harlequin, I would like to surprise Mr. Rawlins by showing him how much I have learned in his absence."

Persis wrinkled her nose. "I don't care for smelly stables. I'll stay here and talk to Mrs. Valerian."

I thought that Seton looked disappointed as I rose to go with him.

At least the stables, some little distance from the house, showed signs of having been recently repaired. There were Negro boys whitewashing the new length of fence around the stable yard, while another, inside, was cleaning and polishing riding gear.

I knew what Persis meant as we stepped through the wide door, for there was a reek of manure, feed and warm horse-flesh in the building that permeated everything. Yet I did not find it unpleasant. Horses were blowing and stomping in their stalls, for the flies were appalling. Seton waved them aside and led me to the largest box stall. I recognized Hamid at once, his chestnut coat glistening like satin, the whites of his eyes showing as he lifted his head in a startled manner at our approach.

Seton spoke to him quietly and touched his nose through the open half-door. Emboldened by his action I put out my fingers too, and timidly rubbed his incredibly soft muzzle. But he tossed his head and drew back, evidently wary of the unfamiliar scent —or perhaps he wasn't used to women. I told Seton this and he laughed.

"I don't think he's ever been close to a woman. He has a lot to learn yet."

"I somehow thought breeding horses were used just for that, not for riding?"

"Most of them *are* kept just for breeding, but we have so few horses, we have to ride ours as well. Come, I'll show you the new mares and fillies."

In adjoining stalls I duly admired the smaller but just as sleek animals, and I had to admit that whatever Clive Valerian might be, he seemed to be an excellent judge of horseflesh.

Afterwards, Seton showed me over some of the plantation, but everywhere I saw signs of disintegration and neglect. I wondered why the Valerians had let everything go so badly. It could not be all due to lack of money. There were still servants on the place, and an effort had been made to salvage the stables, but the rest of the property suffered from what appeared to be pure apathy.

Seton read my glance and flushed slightly under his tan. "Marchmount," he said defensively, "was taken over by Union troops during the war. Mother and I had to leave. It was sometime before Clive could get it back, and by then the taxes took everything we could scrounge."

"I'm sorry," I said, meaning it. "I believe my husband faced a similar problem."

"No," he said slowly, "Harlequin was always different—and so were the Rawlinses." He sounded dejected and weary.

"But now," I replied brightly, hoping to draw him out of his unhappy mood, "you've got the horses again, such beauties. Surely everything will be different."

"Yes, different, but will it be any better?" He gave me a wise, old man look. The war I thought, had truly robbed this boy of his youth and his hopes.

"I'm sure it will be," I replied stoutly, though I wasn't at all certain now that this would be the case.

"May I ask you something?" he said suddenly.

"Why, of course, Seton."

"Is it true that you saw the ghost at Harlequin?"

Whatever I had expected him to say, it had not been this.

"No," I said. "I heard something in my dressing room, and thought I saw something on the wall."

"What was it?"

"I'm—not sure. A stain. But my husband says there is no truth to the old tales and rumors."

His face had grown very pale.

"The blood," he said, "you saw the bloodstain! Very few have seen that. Do you know what it means?"

I was impatient with his questions now. I suddenly agreed with my husband that it was best to forget the whole matter. Whether it was some prank or even some spiritual manifestation, it had not harmed me, and I had no intention of dwelling on it further.

I said, "Seton, I don't want to talk about it, but I do know the legend. Honore told me."

"You know about the—danger it warns of?" His eyes had a gleam in them that I did not like. Truly, superstition was a terrible thing.

"I know about everything," I said firmly, hoping to end the conversation. We were close to the house now.

"It isn't all superstition," he said clearly as if he had read my mind. "Honore believes it."

"She was brought up on the stories."

"No. She—knows. Ask her why it's called Harlequin House, and have her show you the Harlequin Room." He gave me no chance to reply but held the door back abruptly for me to enter the house.

Clive Valerian had not arrived by dinnertime, so we dined in the hot but shadowy dining room served by old Cleta and a young girl, and I struggled to make a show of enjoying the soggy rice and boiled chicken, and wilted salad greens.

We remained an hour longer after the meal, and before we got ready to leave, I issued an invitation to the Valerians to call at Harlequin.

"My health is so poorly," said Mrs. Valerian, "that I no longer go out. But your visit has refreshed me, so do come again soon, and please give Samantha my regards."

We promised to do so, and were on the point of stepping into the carriage when a horse and rider galloped up the drive.

"It's Clive," said Seton.

Mrs. Valerian looked suddenly frustrated.

Clive Valerian threw himself from his steaming horse and tossed the reins to Seton with an imperious gesture. The scowl on his long face smoothed itself out as he recognized us, and was replaced by a tight, amused smile. He touched his moustache and there was an odd light in his yellowish eyes. He made us a flourishing bow, and extended the usual flowery welcome southerners gave visitors in their homes.

He insisted that we return to the house long enough for him to offer us a stirrup cup. This proved to be a very old sherry that he brought out and served himself.

"To your continued health and happiness, ladies, and to a speedy return to Marchmount!"

We sipped sparingly, Persis and I, and I told him how much I had admired the horses Seton had shown me. This seemed to please him, and he asked, "Has your husband got his new animals yet?"

"He is in Kentucky now," I replied, "I have no doubt he will return with them."

"But not with a stud equal to Hamid," he said with the same insolent assurance I had heard in Sam Forbes' voice.

My chin came up; I wanted for some reason to defend my husband and Harlequin from this man. And I found myself wondering, at the same time, why they had fought a duel so long ago.

I said as deliberately as possible, "I'm sure that everything has its price, Mr. Valerian, and that even horses such as Hamid can be bought if one has sufficient funds."

"Yankee traders have always thought that," he said flatly.

"And proved it," I said with spirit. Out of the corner of my eye I could see Mrs. Valerian draw in her breath and press a hand to her breast.

Clive Valerian stood very still regarding me coldly. Suddenly the stem of his wine glass splintered under his fingers and he threw it from him angrily.

"The only thing you've proved in coming here, Mrs. Rawlins," he said in a harsh voice, "is that you intend to flaunt your

wealth in the community, and that Breckenridge Rawlins, damn his soul, has a
hankering for my studs! You came here to
try'n buy him, didn't you?"

I stared at him in startled amazement,
for such a thought had never crossed my
mind.

"Well, all your Yankee dollars won't buy
him, hear? An' if my mother there was
starvin', an' the stud was the last thing I had
on this earth, I wouldn't sell him to a
Rawlins!" He turned away, crunching the
glass under his boot heels as he left the
room.

Mrs. Valerian was weeping softly into
her handkerchief, and Seton, white faced,
stood looking after his brother with his fists
clenched tightly at his sides.

Persis surprised me. Before anyone else
could speak, she said with cool dignity,
"Come Cousin Tamson, it's time we left. We
should never have come here in the first
place." When Seton stepped forward and
opened his mouth to speak she stopped him.
"Don't apologize for your boorish brother,
Seton; everyone knows the sort of man he is.
Don't worry, Cousin Breckenridge need
never know that we were here."

Seton, looking crestfallen but at the
same time relieved, saw us to the carriage in
painful silence. He gave Persis a long, and I
felt, entreating look, and then Jason
whipped up the horses.

Persis only spoke once on our return

journey, and neither her words nor her tone were reassuring to my feelings.

"I hope you've learned a lesson. In the future, only go calling when the head of the house invites you personally, and never go near Clive Valerian again. He hates us, you know—especially Cousin Breckenridge."

"Why?" I asked softly. "Tell me about it."

But she shaded her eyes with her parasol and refused to answer my question, and we rode the rest of the way to Harlequin in silence.

That night as I was getting ready for bed, I asked Honore some of the questions that were bothering me, but she seemed strangely withdrawn and none of her answers were fully satisfying.

I asked her to tell me how Harlequin got its name, and about the Harlequin Room, and she said, "During the Reformation and the persecution of the Catholics, a priest flew to the Rawlins family for protection. He entered the house disguised in a harlequin costume during a fancy dress ball. The Rawlinses hid him in the family chapel, in a secret vault. But he was discovered before he could leave the chapel and executed on the spot. The Rawlinses had the figure of a harlequin painted on the chapel wall in his memory, but there was a bad aura about the place and it was no longer used for family worship."

"And the Harlequin name of course,

stuck to the place?"

She nodded. It all seemed straightforward enough, just some more of the legends of the old house, which might or might not be based on facts.

"Tell me one more thing, Honore," I said, "Why did my husband fight a duel with Clive Valerian?"

A stubborn, closed look came over her face. "I believe Mr. Rawlins is the one to tell you about that, madame. He does not like it mentioned. It was very long ago."

"Honore," I persisted. "Was it—over a woman?"

Her brief nod was almost imperceptible, then she was gone.

What sort of woman, I mused, could have caused my cold, unemotional husband to engage in a duel with Clive Valerian?

Then I gave up the useless question and answer game with myself, and climbed into the high lonely bed of the Rawlins brides.

And later, waking suddenly as I had on that first night, I heard again the sounds of something moving in the dressing room. But this time I did not get up. If it was a spirit in turmoil, as Honore seemed to think, I had no wish to disturb it. If it was human, I was too weary to confront it at the moment. I turned over and went back to sleep.

9

A week later, when I came down to breakfast at my usual early hour, I found my husband standing in the hall waiting for me.

"It's good to see you looking so well, Tamson. I didn't want to disturb you last night when I got in; it was very late. I trust Harlequin wasn't too much for you?"

"No, I rather enjoyed it."

"Good. Shall we go in to breakfast? Afterwards we can talk."

He looked tired but inwardly pleased about something.

We were alone at the small table he had ordered set up on the terrace, as no one else was up yet, and I saw with surprise that there was a tissue wrapped package at my place.

"A remembrance from New Orleans," he said.

"You were in New Orleans?"

"Briefly, to order some things for the

house. They will be here directly. But the horses," his grin widened like that of a small boy, giving him a different appearance, "will be here today. I brought them on the packet with me, but left them with a friend in Charleston, to rest up from the journey. Open your gift."

I untied the pale lavender ribbon that bound it, took off the tissue, and opened the small cardboard box. Inside, on a bed of lavender velvet, was a beautiful amethyst ring, the setting carved to match my wedding band.

I raised my eyes to his in surprise and pleasure. No one had ever given me a jewel of my own before, and the ones I had inherited had never seemed my personal property somehow. "It's very lovely," I said. "Thank you, Breckenridge." His Christian name seemed to come more easily to my lips than usual.

"I didn't give you a betrothal ring," he answered, "and you needn't consider this as one. I hope that when you—leave, you will keep it in friendship, as a memento of Harlequin."

"Of course," I said quickly. "It was most kind and thoughtful of you. I love amethysts."

"Lavender and purple suit you," he replied. "Most women have difficulty wearing those colors, but your skin is so fair and your hair such a pure brown, the colors heighten your features. I would like you know," he added uncomfortably, "this ring was not purchased with—our money. It came from money left from some crops I sold last year. It is from the earnings of Harlequin."

"Thank you," I said, touched by his act. I might even had added more, but the maid appeared to serve us, and he became his usual distant, abrupt self. He was a strange man, I thought, this southerner to whom I was married, however temporarily, and I would never understand him.

After breakfast we went to his office-study, and I showed him the simple records I had kept. He seemed more than satisfied and was warm in his praise of me.

"You found Forbes helpful?" he asked.

I hesitated. "Yes, in the farm work, but I don't like him—I don't trust him somehow."

He seemed amused. "Why not? I know to a woman he must seem crude, not a gentleman, but he knows his job. He wasn't rude to you in any way?" There was a sharper note in his voice.

I didn't answer his question directly. Instead I said, "It is just his attitude about Yankee money."

Breckenridge's face suddenly went still. "When did he mention money to you?"

"He didn't—not directly." I was suddenly flustered under his hawklike gaze. I hadn't known the words would disturb him so much.

"How have you arrived at this conclusion then? Answer me, Tamson."

"It was just a horse," I stammered, "over mention of the expense of good horses. It was nothing really—please don't question me so closely."

"You said a horse first," his voice hammered at me relentless. "Was it the stud Clive Valerian brought from Kentucky?"

I was completely tongue-tied in the face of his icy wrath.

"Was it? Answer me!"

"Yes, it was Hamid," I whispered, under his burning gaze.

I heard him let out an oath, and then he stepped towards me to take my shoulders in an iron grip, and held me stiffly in front of him. "How the devil do you know the stud's name is Hamid? Have you seen him? Was the horse here at Harlequin—was Clive Valerian here?"

His hard bruising hands shook me till my head moved back and forth like a doll's. Breckenridge's anger was a cold frightening thing, much worse even than the violent hatred I had seen Clive Valerian display at Marchmount.

"No!" I managed to get out at last. "No, he wasn't here!"

He released me then and I saw that his face was pale, the lips drawn back against his white teeth.

"Forbes told me about Hamid," I added quickly.

He passed a hand over his eyes. "I'm—sorry, Tamson. I'm overly tired from my journey. But you must realize, from our meeting at Croix, that Valerian and I are not friends."

"Yes," I said, "that was quite clear."

"What did you think of Valerian?" he

asked suddenly.

"I think he is a braggart, but also a dangerous man. He allows his emotions and appetites to rule him, so he would naturally hate those who have self control."

He gave me a quick admiring glance. "That's very discerning of you, my dear. You are a constant surprise to me. One moment I see only the callow schoolgirl, the next a mature woman."

I said with what force I could muster, "Regardless of Mr. Valerian's shortcomings, I don't appreciate the way you have acted!"

"I agree. I did not act like a gentleman, and I apologize. Can you forgive my actions this once? I assure you such a thing will not happen again."

I didn't have time to reply, for a servant girl tapped and entered hurriedly, mumbling, "Please, master, Miss Vinton just arrived, sir. Honore asked me to tell you straight off."

I saw my husband's head jerk up, while a strange emotion I could not decipher washed across his lean face. Was it shock, joy, or some deeper feeling?

"Here?" he asked swiftly, "Here at Harlequin?"

"Yes, sir."

"Very well, we'll be right out."

The girl left, closing the door, and my husband said, "A distant kinswoman of ours. Will you come with me to greet her?"

I nodded and put my hand lightly on the arm he offered. I could feel his arm tremble under my fingers. Whoever this was, her name had produced some powerful emotion in this otherwise taciturn man, and I felt curious to meet her.

In the great hall two women were standing talking, half in shadow, for the vastness of the place never made it seem very light. As we drew closer, I recognized one of the figures as Honore's. The other, still wearing her small modish hat, at first glance looked like a slightly more mature Persis. She was taller, with the same pale oval face and light hair and eyes, but on closer observation the similarity ended. This woman had a longer nose and sharp boned chin, and her narrow eyes were a pale blue like those of a Siamese cat.

Breckenridge stepped forward a pace from me to greet her, and she flung herself into his arms kissing him swiftly on the cheek.

"Breckenridge, dear, it's been such a long time!"

He seemed faintly embarrassed, but continued to hold the two slim hands she thrust into his.

"Rina, this is a great surprise. You're a long way from home. Why didn't you write you were coming. Why, not since the war—"

She stopped him with a finger laid quickly across his lips. "Don't mention a word about that horrid war! I can't bear it. It just got so lonely and borin' there for me all alone at Bellehaven, that I couldn't stand it another minute. When I heard you were back, and with a new bride," her eyes slid swiftly over me, "I simply had to come pay my respects. You don't mind?"

"Certainly not, Rina. You're always welcome at Harlequin. Honore, see about Miss Rina's luggage and room."

"I have already done so, sir." She bowed and turned away, but something in the rigidity of her back told me that something about the arrival of Miss Vinton had displeased her.

"And now," our guest continued in her light, carrying voice, "I must meet your new bride."

My husband turned and said, "Tamson, may I present one of our kinfolk, Miss Corrine Vinton."

Rina swooped forward to kiss me lightly on the cheek. It felt like being brushed by a butterfly's wing, and I caught the scent of jasmine.

"How nice for poor, dear Breckenridge, to have found such a suitable bride, after suffering loneliness for so long."

Her pale lashes veiled her look of bold curiosity, but I saw Breckenridge's mouth tighten slightly at the corners.

"I know what it is to be all alone," pouted Rina. "I simply cannot run Bellehaven all by my poor little self, Breckenridge; that is one reason I've come. I do so need a man's advice."

"I'll be glad to help in any way that I can, Rina."

"I knew you'd say that, dear Breckenridge, you were always so gallantly devoted to—Bellehaven."

Again that strange undecipherable look crossed my husband's face, but the next moment Aunt Samantha and Persis came down the stairs towards us.

They seemed as astonished to see Rina Vinton as Breckenridge had been. Persis even looked a shade angry at the sight of her, but then Persis was unaccountable anyway. In a moment, after a show of hospitable greetings, Aunt Samantha ushered Rina and Persis off to breakfast with her, and Breckenridge and I were momentarily alone.

"You don't object to having a guest for awhile?" he asked diffidently.

I raised my eyebrows. "Why should I? Harlequin belongs to you. I am merely—"

"A paying guest?" he finished for me bitterly.

I felt myself flushing in hot anger.

"Please," he said, "that wasn't fair of me. I —didn't mean it the way it sounded." He ran a lean hand over his face. "I don't know what's the matter with me today. Things—you must forget I said that, Tamson."

"It's all right," I said stiffly polite.

He suddenly reached into an inside pocket and held out a letter, smiling tentatively as if it were a peace offering.

"I forgot to give you this at breakfast. The mail had just come when I got down this morning."

I took it from him and saw that it was from Mrs. Campbell in Boston. I felt suddenly very alone and homesick.

He waited, seeming at a loss for words and said finally, "Please make my excuses to the others. I won't be back to dinner. I have to make arrangements for the horses. But I will be in for supper." He wheeled away from me and went out the front door.

I had no wish to join the ladies, so I went back up to my room, meaning to put away the new ring Breckenridge had given me. Somehow my first pleasure in the gift had been spoiled for me by his subsequent actions. I knew now that he was as violent and unpredictable as ever, and I disliked both traits in a man.

I sat down in front of the fireplace and tore open the letter from Mrs. Campbell, and as I did so a small newspaper clipping fell onto my lap. Curiously, I took it up and began to read, expecting it to be some report on current Boston society. Then as I read, I felt my breath stop suddenly. Everything inside me seemed welded into stark immobility, as my eyes and my mind devoured the words.

Accident To Army Train.
Word has reached Washington that a U.S. Army Column, including women and children as well as troops under Colonel Mason, en route to quarters at Fort Grant, Arizona Territory, was attacked by Apaches, and all but wiped out. A scouting party from the fort, arriving on the scene by accident, was all that saved the few

*survivors. Among those massacred
in the attack was Mrs. John
Markham, late of Boston, nee Lucile
Napier. She and her husband, Captain John Markham, departed only
recently to make their home in the far
west. Captain Markham, though
wounded, survives his wife.*

The print, and then the whole room,
swam in front of my eyes. Lucy, I thought,
poor Lucy lying out there on the prairie,
murdered! And John—the thought took hold
of me like a powerful hand shaking me—John
had been spared. He was alive! Then the guilty
thought followed at once. He was also free. . . .

I put my hands over my eyes and wept in
shamed relief. I didn't want Lucy dead, and in
such a terrible fashion, and I wept for her as
well as for John. But the guilty wanton
thought of John's sudden freedom would not
leave me either. The heart, I thought wildly, is
a betraying, incomprehensible organ, to feel
unhappiness and elation at the same time.

With an effort I forced myself to read Mrs.
Campbell's letter which told in more detail of
the tragedy. John, she wrote, had been badly
injured, given sick leave, and posted to
Washington. My heart gave a lurch when I
realized that according to her letter, he might
already be that close to me.

Aware of the hot blood staining my
cheeks, I took the letter and clipping and went
into the dressing room to cool my burning

face with lotion. I folded the letter and clipping and stowed them in the jewel case John had given me. I dared not let myself think that after a decent interval, perhaps when we both were free, we might see each other again. Then I heard someone tap at the door, and I made a mighty effort to control my thoughts and my emotions.

"Come in," I said lightly, and Honore entered the room with a grave look on her face.

"Miss Samantha asks if you are free to join the ladies for a short drive before dinner, madame?"

"Of course," I said, "will you get my pink parasol and hat please, Honore?"

"Yes, madame."

I watched her select the things from the wardrobe, adding a reticule and gloves of pink silk, but noted the slowness and preoccupation of her movements, and wondered what was bothering her.

"Honore," I said, "has Miss Vinton been at Harlequin often in the past?"

She stiffened for a moment, and then said in her perfect diction, "Yes, madame. In the old days she and her sister were frequent visitors. They are distant Rawlins kinfolk."

"Her sister? But surely Miss Vinton said she was alone at—Bellehaven?"

"Miss Rena is alone now, the others of the family are all dead."

"The war?" I asked.

Honore nodded but did not speak further.

She helped me with my things, adding, "Have a good drive, madame."

As I was drawing on my gloves, I asked suddenly on impulse, "Honore, someday will you show me the Harlequin Room?"

Her dark eyes widened, grew enormous, the white showing around the edges. "This is not a place for you, madame, unless the master himself has said—"

"No," I cut in quickly, "I did not mention our talks to him."

"Then I cannot show it to you. But I assure you, there is nothing there—now."

"But why shouldn't you take me to see it? My husband told me I was free to go anywhere in this house."

"I cannot take you to the Harlequin Room unless he instructs me to do so, madame," she said stubbornly. She was shaking slightly, her lips unsteady. "Please do not ask me."

"Very well, Honore," I said primly, "I will ask him instead."

She folded her arms and bowed slightly. "Of course, madame, that will be best."

She looked as enigmatic as a sphinx, but I felt she was troubled all the same.

Jason had the carriage in the front drive, and my husband was just helping Rina Vinton into it when I arrived. Aunt Samantha, with her green parasol already open, was seated facing the back of the driver, and Rina sat down beside her. When Breckenridge helped me in I took the seat opposite them.

"Enjoy your drive, ladies," he told all of

us.

"Dear Breckenridge," cooed Rina, "How tiresome that you can't go with us."

"My loss, I assure you, Rina," he replied politely and again there was that unreadable look on his dark face.

Aunt Samantha had evidently instructed Jason to drive towards Charleston, for he turned in that direction.

"Why didn't Persis come?" I asked as we drove down the tree-lined road.

"A dreadful headache, my dear," replied Aunt Samantha quickly. "She's subject to them, poor child, like all Malots. My own dear mother had to take to her bed for days."

"And I have heard," interjected Rina sympathetically, "that like Mrs. Rawlins, Breckenridge's mother, these attacks often followed their husbands' sessions at the race-track or the gaming tables?"

Aunt Samantha compressed her lips and changed the subject.

I fell to studying the landscape, bored with their gossip about people I did not know. The exotic tropical vegetation fascinated me, with red birds darting like fireflies through the palmetto and live oak branches, festooned with whispery moss, and every now and then the hauntingly beautiful trill of a mockingbird. North of this region, Breckenridge had told me, were great stands of pine trees and mountains, though I doubted if they were like the soaring White Mountains of my own part of the country. Here and there, as the road turned, I caught a glimpse of a stream, no doubt on its way to join the Ashley or Cooper on their way to the sea at Charleston.

Slowly, I became aware that Aunt Samantha had asked me a question, and that both of my companions were looking at me awaiting my reply.

"I'm sorry," I said lamely, "I didn't hear what you were saying. I must have been daydreaming—please forgive me."

Aunt Samantha waved a plump hand and smiled, "All brides daydream, my dear. What Rina wanted to know was when you plan to hold the ball and reception at Harlequin? She must stay for it of course."

Rina was watching me intently, her pale blue eyes slightly narrowed.

"I—I had forgotten all about the ball," I stammered. And it was true. In Breckenridge's absence, with so much to do, it had slipped my mind. "I suppose anytime would do now that my husband has returned."

For the past few weeks I knew both Aunt Samantha and Persis had spent a part of each day with the seamstresses who had come to the house from Charleston, to work on the new fabrics I had bought them. Their new wardrobes must be nearing completion.

"Breckenridge," I hesitated only slightly over his name, but I felt that Rina caught the trace of uncertainty in my tone, "told me he has purchased some new things for the house. Perhaps he would prefer us to wait until they have arrived."

Aunt Samantha leaned forward and put her hand over mine.

"Tamson, my dear, when will you learn that you are now the mistress of Harlequin? The social calendar of Harlequin has always been at the discretion of its mistress—*not* its master. Running the plantation is one thing, but the running of the household is another."

"Well," I said, not liking to be forced into a corner by the two women, but realizing that I must make some sort of acceptable reply, "this is Thursday, I think I should like it a week from Saturday. Will that give everyone enough notice?"

"Oh, yes!" cried Aunt Samantha. "And Persis and Rina and I will help you write out the invitations. How wonderful this is going to be! We must ask just everyone around; no one must be forgotten."

"Except the Valerians," said Rina softly.

Aunt Samantha's face grew red. "Well, of course we can't ask the Valerians. Breckenridge would never permit it."

"That's true," said Rina thoughtfully, "but actually the guest list is in Tamson's hands, isn't it?"

I knew she was deliberately issuing me a challenge, though I did not know why, unless she hoped I would make a fool of myself both as a Yankee and as mistress of Harlequin. But I felt my chin go up as New England contrariness took possession of me.

"My husband," I said coldly, "has forbidden the war to be mentioned in our house and

I share his feelings to a degree, but I also feel it is high time old enmities were forgotten, on all sides. Persis and I recently called on Mrs. Valerian at Marchmount. I found her quite charming. And young Mr. Seton Valerian lunched—took dinner with us at Harlequin not long ago."

Aunt Samantha looked uncomfortable, and Rina seemed frankly awed. It was not what she had expected, I could see.

"If I choose to invite the Valerians," I continued smoothly, "I know Breckenridge would join me in extending our hospitality to them."

I was not sure of any such thing. In fact I knew it would probably end up quite the contrary. Breckenridge would be furious with me. But on the other hand I was equally certain that none of the Valerians would accept my invitation. It was more than a safe gamble, and perhaps my husband need never find out that I had sent them an invitation.

Rina, I saw, looked suddenly pale and defeated. I was enjoying my triumph, and turned to nod to a passing horseman who had raised his hat to our carriage hardly troubling to look at him.

It was Rina who cried out, "Seton—speak of the devil, it's Seton Valerian! My heavens, how you have grown!"

Seton, for it was indeed he, drew alongside on a lean gray horse, his young face puzzled. Jason, out of courtesy, had halted the carriage.

"Don't you remember me, Seton?" Rina asked. "But of course I was only at Marchmount twice, and you were just a child. You knew my sister, Anabelle, better."

His face flushed at her words and he nearly dropped his hat.

"Then—you must be Miss Rina Vinton?"

"Go to the head of the class!" Rina laughed, and added, "You are all grownup. We were just talking about you, Seton. Mrs. Rawlins is giving a ball a week from this Saturday, she intends to invite you and your family."

Seton looked back at her in a bewildered fashion, and I decided this had gone far enough. It was after all, to be *my* ball and should be up to me to issue the invitations.

"Of course," I said smoothly, "after our pleasant visit, Persis' and mine, at your lovely Marchmount the other day, your family was the first I thought of, Seton. I know so few neighbors as yet myself. You will of course receive a written invitation, but I hope that you can assure me now that your family will honor Harlequin by their presence?"

He seemed tongue-tied, but managed to get out that his mother accepted no social engagements these days due to her delicate health, and that his brother Clive was away a great deal on business. He was striving valiantly to make his escape, when I noted that another rider had come to a halt in the shadows of an oak tree across the road.

Rina, glancing in the same direction,

went very white, and from under her parasol
Aunt Samantha let out a frightened squeak.
On closer inspection I saw that it was Clive
Valerian, reining the Arab, Hamid, towards us
as he doffed his hat.

"Ladies," he greeted us in that cold,
deadly drawl that I had come to hate, "you
have brightened my day by your presence."
As his eyes met Rina's, she lowered her lashes
swiftly as if to avoid the sight of him sitting his
horse there in the bright sunlight. "This *is* a
surprise! Good afternoon, Miss Rina."

"G-Good afternoon, Mr. Valerian," she
murmured.

"You're a long way from home, Miss Rina.
But you came no doubt to revel in the newly
found abundance of Harlequin?"

Aunt Samantha said breathlessly. "How
can you talk like that, Clive—where are your
manners?"

"I beg your pardon, Miss Samantha. I
regret to inform you that I lost them in the war
—amongst a great many other things." He
turned his insolent gaze on me. "So you are
giving a great ball in the old Harlequin
tradition, Mrs. Rawlins?" There was an implied
insult in the words.

I felt two hot spots of color on my cheeks,
but I continued to return his gaze steadily.
"That is correct, Mr. Valerian. However, you
had no right to eavesdrop."

He raised his brows. "It is not my fault
that you did not hear me ride up. I was only a
short ways behind my brother. But of course in

deference to Hamid's still unshod hooves, I was riding him on the grass verge, which deadened the sound of our approach. Now that we are all so happily met, I would like to add an apology for my personal actions during your recent visit to Marchmount, Mrs. Rawlins. I was—not quite myself."

"I understand," I found myself answering coldly.

He sat the restless stallion studying me. "You know, I may have entirely underestimated you, Mrs. Rawlins. Perhaps I'm beginning to understand how you Yankees won the war. You charge in where angels fear to tread, just as a matter of course, don't you? Damned if I don't admire you for it, but it won't work, you know. Not here among our bloody but unbowed gentry. We may be rotting in our crumbling mansions, ma'am, but the old dauntless pride still holds sway. Pride, as you doubtless know, was Satan's own sin. But it makes up for a great many—losses. Good afternoon, Mrs. Rawlins—ladies." He put spurs to his mount and galloped off, and the sound of his derisive laughter floated back to us as sharp as a driver's whip on the backs of startled horses.

Seton was scarlet faced with shame as he struggled to apologize. "You must forgive my brother, Mrs. Rawlins—ladies. He—he says these things without thinking."

"Think nothing of it, Seton," I said. "We shall look forward to seeing you at the ball."

"Thank you, ma'am."

I gave Jason orders to drive on, and we left poor Seton still sitting his horse with his hat in his hand. I was reflecting that he seemed to have enough troubles without the added burden of a sadistic brother like Clive Valerian, and for the first time in my life I felt hatred for another human being. I found myself wondering also what deep enmity lay between my husband and Clive Valerian. In any case, I intended to mail an invitation to my ball to the Valerians of Marchmount, to spite Rina Vinton if nothing else. And then my thoughts turned to other things. John Markham was back! And he was free. I refused to let myself dwell on memories of Lucy. And suddenly my heart soared like the flaming redbirds in the trees.

10

That evening at supper, my husband was much gayer and more amiable than I had ever seen him, and I put it down to Rina Vinton's presence. He was most attentive to her, and they seemed to share an understanding that went beneath the surface of their conversations. It was natural, I decided, since they had probably grown up together, though I was surprised to learn that Rina was only a few years older than I was. I wondered if Breckenridge had ever been in love with her, if perhaps he still was. If such was the case, I thought, in due time he would be free to marry her, and Harlequin would have its proper mistress at last. On the other hand, Breckenridge had been rather cold-blooded and ruthless in his methods of providing for his first love, but then he was that kind of man. Even Rina, I thought, could never hope to come before Harlequin.

After the meal, when the others had retired to the drawing room for coffee and to listen to Persis play the piano, I followed my husband to the study and tapped on the door. He had excused himself shortly before dessert on the plea that he had some urgent work to catch up on.

"Come in," he called. His voice sounded irritable.

I opened the door and found him seated at his desk with an open ledger in front of him. He seemed surprised at my entrance. "May I see you for a moment?" I asked.

"Of course." He rose and led me to a chair in front of the empty fireplace, but he continued to stand, one arm resting along the mantel.

"I've decided," I said, "to give the ball a week from next Saturday, if that will meet with your approval?"

"Suit yourself," he replied carelessly. "You don't need to consult me about such things. Aunt Samantha and Persis can help you with the guest list, if that is what is bothering you. As for the other arrangements, Honore will provide whatever you require. You don't need to bother me with things like this."

"I wasn't aware," I said stiffly, "that this would bother you."

He straightened up. "Of course I didn't mean it the way it sounds. It's only that I have so many things on my mind now—I've only the rest of this year, you know, to make good and pay you back your money. Will you excuse my rudeness on that account?" He smiled down at me, and the smile softened and changed his face, making it seem momentarily almost as boyish as Seton's.

I said quickly, "If you need more time to repay the loan, you know you can have it."

The smile left his face as swiftly as it had come. His voice sounded harsh, "I would never have accepted the money in the first place if I had not intended to repay every penny of it in the time specified, and I can do it. I am certain of that. Forbes has shown me today that the crops are prospering, and now with the new horses and hired hands, there should be no difficulty. Harlequin is coming back into its own."

"I know how you feel about Harlequin," I answered, "I—I grew very fond of it too, in your absence. I really know very little about farms or plantations, but aren't there always risks to consider, such as drought and insect damage?"

"Of course." He scowled down at me. "But I have seen no signs of anything like that, and please God, I won't. In any case leave the problems of the plantation to me. Whatever happens you will be paid in full at the end of the year, I guarantee that, even if I have to sell more land."

"But surely that would be foolhardy," I found myself arguing. "If you sell more land, you won't have enough left for Harlequin to carry itself. Mr. Forbes told me that you are down to a minimum acreage now."

"Forbes," he said through clenched teeth, "is a fool; he had no right discussing such matters with you."

I was suddenly furious with him. "I'm not one of your sheltered southern belles," I said, "who has to be shielded from life's realities. In the north women know about their husbands' businesses, often help run them, but that doesn't make them any the less women. You have a silly out-moded idea here in the south about a woman's place and duties—why it's like purdah amongst the Moslems. I think it's selfish and presposterous!"

"Are you finished?" he asked in a deadly cold voice.

I got to my feet. "Quite, thank you. As a matter of fact, I've decided that after the ball I will be leaving Harlequin."

My words seemed to take him by complete surprise, deflating him and wiping out his anger completely.

"You're—leaving?"

"I didn't promise to live here the whole year. You yourself told me that I might travel if I chose."

He passed a hand over his face and didn't speak for a moment. Then he said, "I —I wish you wouldn't go just yet, Tamson, even though you hate it here and plainly find me intolerable. I regret that, though I suppose it was inevitable. But that is beside the point. I know I haven't the right to ask more of you," he smiled wryly, "but you have just depicted our southern society only too well. We are behind the times, I suppose—tradition and habit die hard. I do not minimize the fact that the whole south has a long struggle ahead of it. I only want to make sure that Harlequin at least, wins that struggle."

"What are you trying to say?" I was bewildered by his words, but I had no intention of granting him any more favors.

He sighed. "I'm trying to tell you that when you live here, you must live at the same pace as the others or you can't hope to survive—until some great changes take place, and that can only come gradually. I've made personal agreements with other planters and business men, on the strength of their belief in Harlequin, and their trust in me. A family upset, a scandal—separation, before the end of the first year of my marriage, could destroy all that."

"But you knew that I might not remain here during the entire year." I felt angry with him and frustrated.

"If you would only wait for six months at least, I could then perhaps explain your absence as due to illness, or the need for a change of climate, and there would be no need for announcing our—separation—until the end of the year. By that time most of my commitments will have been settled. You did promise to give me a year?"

His words seemed sincere enough. I really did not understand the south and its ways. It could all be just as he claimed, but on the other hand, I did not intend to be held at Harlequin. John was home and he was free. I had to see him. Answering Breckenridge, I tried to make my tone reasonable. "What difference will it make if I leave now and you give out the same excuse of my illness and sudden need of change?"

"It would be too soon," he argued. "Everyone would suspect at once that there was something wrong between us. A bride doesn't pack up and leave her husband's house a few weeks after her arrival, or even a few months after—unless there is something very wrong."

I could see that by his code the situation would be difficult to explain. I bit my lip and said slowly, "Very well, I'll think it over, but I haven't made up my mind as yet. I can't promise anything."

His tone changed again, became almost humble. "Have you been so dreadfully unhappy at Harlequin?"

"No," I said truthfully, "not really unhappy. It's just that I feel—out of place. Not that everyone hasn't been kind—"

"Everyone but me," he ended bitterly, adding on a lower note, "you must hate me very much."

"I don't hate you," I said dispassionately, "though I realize I'm far from understanding you. I appreciate what you are trying to do for Harlequin, but you go about it all wrong. You should pay at least as much attention to the people involved as to the land itself."

A look of sudden curiosity flickered in his dark eyes. "You doubt that I have their welfare at heart?"

I waved a hand impatiently. "The physical interest, yes, but what do you know about them as individuals? Persis, for instance. She is a very unhappy young girl."

"Persis?" He seemed genuinely astonished. "Persis is better off than most young southern girls at this time."

"Being better off," I said, "does not necessarily insure happiness. I know from experience. All my material desires were provided for, too, but I knew no real happiness until—"

His eyes watched me with a burning steadiness. "Until you met John Markham?"

"Yes."

"I don't suppose you will ever forget him?"

"No. I won't forget him."

His lips twisted sardonically, "You must know it's no use living in the dead past? I hate folly and waste, and for you, thoughts of Markham are sheer waste. As for Persis, if you mean I should provide for her with a John Markham, I'm afraid I can't do that."

"I think that she has already found one of her own, if you will leave her alone."

He was instantly alert. "What's that you say? Who is he? She seldom leaves Harlequin, and we've been in no position to entertain. And before she was away at school. How can there be anyone?"

"I think she is very fond of Seton Valerian, though she won't let herself admit it, because for some reason you seem to hate the entire family."

His shoulders had gone taut, his face lengthened into a cold mask. "Persis will have nothing to do with Seton Valerian. And how do you know anything of Seton? You've never even seen him."

I decided that I might as well have this out with him now.

"I have met all of the Valerian family," I said quietly, "Persis and I made a call at Marchmount in your absence."

"You—what?"

"Seton came here to lunch—to dinner, once. That was when I saw the stallion, Hamid. Seton invited us to call, and we did so the following day. I saw nothing wrong in it. Mrs. Valerian is a sweet and lovely woman, and Seton is a charming boy. Why should they be punished for some fued you share with Clive Valerian?"

"And the estimable Clive," he drawled, "did he welcome you with open arms too?"

"No. It was quite apparent he resented our being there, but his actions could be blamed on the fact that he had been drinking."

"Had he, by God?"

"Yes, but we ignored that fact. I intend to issue the family an invitation to the ball." I said the last deliberately, to remind him that social matters were now in my hands.

He turned away from me towards the empty fireplace, his hands knotted tightly on the mantleshelf, and I thought for a moment I saw them tremble. "No Valerian," he said hoarsely, "has crossed the threshold of Harlequin since—"

"Since you fought a duel with Clive Valerian?" I finished for him.

He whirled to face me, his eyes flashing dangerously. "We don't discuss that in this house. Aunt Samantha had no right—"

"Your women seem to enjoy so few rights," I said scathingly, "not even that of free speech."

For an instant I thought he was going to strike me. Then slowly, the hot color receded from his face and his eyes grew dull.

"I suppose," he said in a tired voice, "you feel now that you have a right to hear the whole story?"

I shook my head. "Not unless you wish to tell me. These matters do not concern me. I am not, after all, really your wife."

"You are my wife, by all that's legal," he answered sharply, "for one year. Maybe you do have a right to hear the story, though it's not a pretty one. But I suppose it's better coming from me, than for you to poke and pry among the gossips."

"I do not poke and pry!" I cried. "And I loathe gossips!"

He came forward in one stride, took me

by the shoulders and pushed me down firmly into the chair.

"Will you shut up for once and listen!"

I was so amazed by his action that I sat speechless staring up at him.

He ran a hand through his dark hair and stepped back to lean against the fireplace. "It was a long time ago, before the war. Clive and I were friends then. We were young and careless and had no responsibilities. I had not recognized the cruel streak in him then.

"He was often at Harlequin, and so was —a certain young lady, of whom we were both very fond. I had no idea that he had been dallying with her, making her believe he was in love with her, until one day she disappeared. Later we found that she had drowned herself in the river. She had left a pitiful note behind, accusing Clive of leading her on and then going back on his word.

"When I showed him the note he merely laughed, and told me she shouldn't have been such a little fool. Since she was related in a distant way, and I had been very fond of her, I felt it my duty to defend her honor. I challenged Valerian to a duel.

"It was the usual sort of thing; we met one morning down by the river where she had died. Valerian was no coward, I will give him that. He fired first and nicked me in the arm, then he stood like a statue waiting for my shot, that devilish cold smile on his face. I fired and hit him in the shoulder, smashing it. He wanted to continue to the death, and we had agreed, but our seconds talked us out of it! Valerian was badly hurt and I realized my satisfaction—and her honor, had been avenged. It was better to let him live with the disgrace that would cling to his name wherever he went in the south. That's what he hates me for, that I didn't kill him, only maimed him. That arm is not much use to him now. And there you have the whole story, and you see why no Valerian can ever come here."

"I'm glad you told me," I said quietly, "and I'm glad you didn't kill Clive Valerian. But I don't agree with you that the breach between you should include the others who are innocent."

He spoke impatiently. "You don't understand these things. I didn't expect that you would. It's a waste of time talking to you!"

"On the contrary, I think I understand you better now than I did before. Did you—love her very much?"

His eyes widened in surprise. "Love? I suppose I did, in a way—as young men idealize an image. But that has nothing to do with matters as they stand now."

"But it has," I said. "I understand now. I thought you were cold, heartless if you like. Now I find that you are capable of love, that you did love once. I'm glad of that. It makes you more—human, don't you see?"

"That's how you've always thought of me," he mused, "cold, heartless, inhuman?"

I flushed. "How could I help it? You've

never shown me any other side."

"I suppose," he spoke slowly, weighing his words, "that's how I must have seemed to you. Believe me that was not my intention."

"It really doesn't matter. I'm sorry you've suffered so."

Suddenly he put back his head and laughed. "Suffered? You really do have the damndest imagination." He glanced down at my hands, and asked abruptly, "Where is the ring I gave you?"

"In my room."

"You don't like it?"

"It's very beautiful. But it's a trifle large, and I was afraid I might lose it somewhere."

"Go and get it, I will have it fixed."

"But surely there is no hurry—"

"Go and get it," he commanded in his old imperious way, then softened the words with a crooked smile, "I want to show you something—please?"

It was the first time he had used that gentle tone with me. He might be John Markham, speaking to me over the dinner table in Boston. And in my own new happiness, knowing I would see John soon, I could afford to be generous to this strange, enigmatic man.

"Very well," I agreed. "I'll only be a moment."

"I'll meet you in the upper hall," he said mysteriously.

11

When I came out of my room a short while later, the ring on my finger, he was standing in the hall waiting for me with a lighted candle in a candlestick. He grinned down at me and said, "A bit of gossip reaches my ears, too, Mrs. Rawlins. I've heard that you are curious about the Harlequin Room?"

Mystified by his behavior I said, "Yes, I have wanted to see it, but Honore told me—"

"That it was forbidden unless the master took you there? That has been the tradition. But come along, you shall see it now."

It seemed to me afterwards that we climbed endless stairs, going down others, through a labyrinth of crooked passageways with numerous closed doors along the way. There were only a few narrow windows and I could see nothing through them but the blackness of the night and I sensed we were very high up in the old house. Our footsteps creaked on ancient timbers, and there was a closed stuffy smell as if these corridors had lain sealed off in time since the days of the Tudors. Who and what, I wondered, had walked along these passages in the past? I felt my palms grow cold and clammy as my husband led me forward towards the place where an ancient murder had been committed, and suddenly I knew that I did not want to see the Harlequin Room at all.

"We're nearly there," said Breckenridge, and even his strong voice sounded hushed and muffled in these silent airless walls.

He paused at last before a thick oak door with heavy iron hinges. A large cross had been carved deeply in the wood. He unlocked the door using a key attached to his watch chain, and pressed down on the latch. Suddenly we both heard a ghostly rustling inside. I drew in my breath and laid my hand on his arm.

He was grinning down at me, "Only mice, Tamson, come on."

I lifted my hand from his arm as he thrust the door open, and reluctantly stepped by him into the airless room.

There were no windows, and it was completely black except for the candle my husband now placed on a table near the heavy door. By its flickering light I studied the Harlequin Room with open curiosity.

It was longer than it was wide, perhaps

twenty-five feet by twelve, with a stone flagged floor and what appeared to be a small stone altar at the other end. Except for some oak benches and the table by the door, it was empty of furnishings. On one wall a large faded tapestry, depicting a Biblical scene, reached nearly to the floor. Behind it, as Breckenridge went to pull it back, I saw a lifesize painting of a man's figure dressed in a harlequin costume. The eyes seemed alive behind the diamond mask, and there was a grimace as of mortal pain on the painted lips. Next to it was a small, arched door built into the worm-eaten frame.

"Well," said Breckenridge, "nothing so terrible to see, is there?"

I shook my head, but my palms still felt clammy, and some aura of the room's dark past, or perhaps just my overwrought imagination, made we want to leave the place.

Breckenridge dusted off one of the benches with his handkerchief, and invited me to sit down. I did so warily, disliking the room more each minute. He sat down beside me and surprised me by reaching for my hand. I attempted to draw it back but he held it firmly, then he removed my amethyst ring and held it up to the light.

"In the very old days," he said, "this was of course the family chapel. All great houses had them, where visiting priests could come to say Mass. Marriages, christenings, and burials were often conducted here. And without fail, here the Master of Harlequin always pledged his troth to his intended bride, and presented her with her ring. Even my own father followed the tradition; it is supposed to seal the bargain irrevocably. And every Harlequin bride is entitled to this honor."

"Even that poor bride who threw herself from the window of—my room?" I whispered.

He looked at me sharply. "Superstition again, I've never believed there was much truth to that legend—but yes, even she."

I shivered slightly though the room was warm. "There was a murder committed here—a priest?"

"Yes. But the Rawlinses were not the murderers. They had tried to hide him over there," he nodded towards the tapestry. "Afterwards they ceased using the room as a chapel, but Rawlins women still received their betrothal rings here."

"Under the circumstances it seems so macabre; I shouldn't think any bride would—"

He broke in impatiently. "I know you don't approve of our—customs. But I wanted to give you your ring—this one, in here as a memento of your brief term as a Harlequin bride. If you really object I'll take you away at once. Do you?"

"I—no, of course not. But this isn't necessary, I'm not really entitled to all the traditions of this house."

"I disagree. Any Harlequin bride, no

matter what her status, is entitled to them. It would please me to present this ring to you in the old way."

"Very well," I said, aware only of an intense desire to get away from the place.

He took my ring in his fingers and went to place it briefly on the altar where he bowed his head once, and then walked back to me. He raised my left hand gently, with its carved gold wedding band winking in the candlelight, and slipped the amethyst on my finger next to it.

He said simply, "With this ring I pledge my troth, lands and holdings, and the honor of Harlequin." He touched the back of my hand briefly with his lips and released it. "You are now," he said solemnly, "full mistress of all that comprises Harlequin."

I was at a loss to know what to say. I had been touched by the beauty and simplicity of the little ceremony, but it was difficult to read the watchful waiting expression in his eyes. I felt uncomfortable, and suddenly wary.

"I—I'm deeply honored," I said haltingly, "to be part of the old tradition. And thank you for showing me the Harlequin Room. It's very interesting, but please try to understand, you will have another wife, and I feel it should be her right rather than mine to receive this declaration from you."

He stood still for a moment looking down at me.

"You no doubt think me as strange a

man as Harlequin is a house?"

"Not—strange," I replied, trying not to offend him, "I suppose it's just that we are so different in upbringing and in outlook."

"Are we really so different?"

"Yes," I said, "we are."

"Tell me, what is it you want out of life, Tamson?" He seemed to have a genuine interest in my answer.

I thought at once of John Markham, and felt myself blush. To cover it I answered brusquely, "Happiness, a home, a family, a useful place in the world as an individual— the things most woman want."

"And you've found none of these things here?" There was a strange irony in his words.

"That's not quite true. I'm very fond of Harlequin, it's beautiful in its own right, and I appreciate the care and veneration that has been given it down through the years. No place kept with such devotion and esteem could be anything but admirable. I like your aunt and Persis, and Honore has been overly kind to me."

He seemed relieved and gave me a warm smile. "I'm glad. It would not have done for you to be wretched here. You have definite plans for your life—after you leave here?"

I glanced down at my hands to avoid his gaze. The amethyst winked like a brilliant lavender eye in the flickering light. "I will go back to Boston, to the Campbells, first."

"You've been homesick?"

"No," I answered truthfully, "not really. I've had no real home for so many years— outside of the boarding school."

He spoke quickly, "Then why go? Harlequin won't always be as dull as it has been these past weeks. You could learn to enjoy it, and you do belong here whether you realize it or not. Look at the splendid job you did managing the plantation while I was away. I—we need you here, Tamson. You could have your place as an individual, an honored and cherished place."

When I glanced up his eyes searched mine with a waiting, guarded expression in their depths. Then before I could answer, he took my shoulders in his hands and drew me slowly towards him. I was too surprised to resist.

"I know," he was saying, "I must seem an unpredictable person to you at times, but I assure you my emotions do not fluctuate. I wanted you from the moment I first saw you at that Inn in Boston, with John Markham. I love you, Tamson, and I shall never love another woman. There can never be another mistress of Harlequin while I live. I have ceased caring whether you could ever love me or not; it will be enough for me to have you here. I—am not always the harsh task-master you seem to think I am. There is another side of me that few people have ever seen. I could show that side to you."

I was not only shocked by his rushing

words, but held speechless in astonishment. Thoughts whirled in my head like pinwheels shooting off useless sparks, and I felt limp under his hands. Before I could gather my wits he bent his head and kissed me gently on the lips, then holding me closer, kissed me again with a fire and challenge that made the blood pound in my head, while I fought desperately to push away from him.

He freed me at once as he felt my struggles. I nearly tottered and fell, but his strong hand reached out and steadied me.

"You—you had no right to do that!" I gasped. I still felt as if the breath had been knocked out of me.

"I had every right to tell you how I felt," he said. "But if my embrace offended you, I'm sorry. But love is not a passive emotion, Tamson. Or didn't you really know? Did Markham always kiss you in a decorous gentlemanly fashion?"

I didn't like his drawling remarks or the slightly triumphant note I detected in his voice. Dear heaven, I thought, I really do hate him.

"Mr. Markham," I said icily, "never offended me by forcing his attentions on me. He always treated me as a gentleman should; that is only one of the reasons I— loved him."

"More fool he, then," said Breck-enridge. "Marriage based on such rigid respect doesn't last."

"How would you know?" I spat the

words out, detesting his smug superiority.

"Because the couple begin by taking each other for granted. There are no surprises, and pretty soon they become bored and then merely resigned. And under that prim little exterior, Tamson, you're no mealymouthed puritan. You've just proven that."

I could feel the heat rising in my face and I was trembling with impotent rage. "You," I choked on the word, "are a despicable cad and no gentleman, for all your fine background, Breckenridge Rawlins!"

"Now you have flicked me on the raw," he said in mock sorrow. "Just because ice water doesn't flow in my veins is no valid proof that I am any the less a gentleman. My intentions were, and are, genuine and honorable." His tone dropped a notch and he said seriously, "I do love you, Tamson. That much you must believe."

I turned away from him, loathing even the sound of his voice. He had upset me, humiliated me, and I hated him more for that than for the deliberate chicanery he had used to get me to marry him. But I had an ace of my own; I could hurt him just as much in return. He believed John Markham was beyond my reach, but he was back and he was free! I had never been a vindictive person, but his actions and words had stripped me bare, it seemed, of even my own personality. At some moment when he kissed me, he had robbed me of something I felt I would never regain.

I turned suddenly and faced him in that room of flickering shadows, where murder had been committed so long ago. Some memory or feeling of the evil deed seemed to envelop me. My hands were clenched at my sides and I could feel the amethyst cutting into my palm as the loose ring turned on my finger where he had placed it.

"I've never loved anyone but John," I cried, "and I never will! I intend to go to him as quickly as possible!"

His brows rose. "To a married man? This is unworthy of you, my dear."

"He is back in Washington. And he is free!"

He stood perfectly still staring at me, his dark face was like a mask. "That—can't be true."

"It is," I assured him triumphantly; "I had a letter and a newspaper clipping from Mrs. Campbell. You handed me the letter yourself."

His eyes were black, fathomless as stygian pits. Then a flicker of pain and loss flashed into their depths and was gone almost instantly. He gave me a crooked smile, bowing slightly, and said, "My congratulations, madame. I—"

But his words were cut off as the door burst open and Honore stood staring at us, holding a lighted lamp in her quivering hands.

"Master! I've hunted high and low for

you. You must come at once. The fields are on fire, and Forbes is afraid the stables may go!"

Breckenridge leaped forward to take the lamp from her. "See that Mrs. Rawlins gets back to her room safely."

"Yes, sir," said Honore, and I could see that under her *cafe-au-lait* skin she was pale with fear.

"Is it so bad?" I asked when he had gone.

"Yes, madame, I fear so. All of Harlequin may go. Come, we must get below, I will be needed."

"But surely I can help too?" I said.

Honore did not answer but picked up the candlestick, shielding the flame with her long palm.

"You had warning of disaster when you first arrived—the blood in your dressing room," she said. "Now it has come. I am afraid—I am much afraid."

The whites shone for a moment around her dark eyes, and I could think of no reply as I followed her out of that eerie room. I felt again that I had lost something there, something that would make me different from that moment on, and I bitterly resented it. I meant never to set foot in the place again; I even found myself wishing that it would be consumed in flames and my memories with it.

12

Afterwards, I could never recall clearly the details of that horrible night.

By the time Honore and I reached the lower halls we could smell the acrid smoke, and see the flames, like molten lava, spreading over the fields and pastures of Harlequin. Like fiery tongues lapping up every living thing in their wake, they came steadily forward.

Aunt Samantha and Persis, dressed in wrappers, stood on the terrace watching and wringing their hands.

"What a terrible thing!" wailed Aunt Samantha. "Dear heaven, what a terrible thing! But they've sent word to all the neighbors; help will be coming soon. If only they aren't too late! Persis dear, do run and get my smelling salts, I feel faint."

We got her into a chair and Persis said, "I'm going to change and see what I can do to help."

"I'll go, too," I said before she disappeared.

While we waited for Persis to return, I stood surveying the scene. Through the dense smoke the area appeared to be alive with shouting, rushing figures armed with buckets and blankets or sacks, attempting to put out the flames. Others seemed to be digging ditches frantically behind the stables. I wondered if they had gotten all the horses out.

There were men pouring down the drive on horseback, too, riding wildly to join the fire fighters.

"How on earth did it start?" I asked.

Aunt Samantha was fanning herself weakly. "No one knows, dear. This can ruin Breckenridge; it could mean the end of Harlequin."

Oh, no, I thought, I did not want to see Harlequin ravaged and lost, no matter what my feelings towards its owner. But I knew her words were true. All that Breckenridge had striven and hoped for, all he had borrowed from me and from others, was going up in smoke before our very eyes.

When Persis returned she had Rina with her.

"Good heavens," said Rina, "I slept right through it all; I didn't know a thing till Persis woke me. Whatever will poor Breckenridge do now?"

"I don't know," moaned Aunt Samantha, sniffing tearfully at the smelling salts Persis had handed her. "This is such a dreadful nightmare."

That was exactly how it seemed, I thought, like a tormented, macabre nightmare that would vanish on awakening. And yet I knew that even if they succeeded in stopping the holocaust, tomorrow would be a day of dire reckoning for all of us.

I went with Persis when she left, first to the big kitchen where Honore kept the maids busy carrying buckets of drinking water and trays of sandwiches out to the fire fighters. On the long kitchen table she had laid out her medicine kit, piles of clean linen and basins of hot water. She was making up a small basket of these same items when we came in.

"How can we help, Honore?" I asked quickly.

She gave me an appraising glance. "Carry these things to old Molly in the servants' quarters; she will know what to do. I will remain here to doctor the white gentlemen, as I am more skillful than she is. There will be many in need of care tonight. I need the maids here, but Persis knows where to go. You are not afraid, madame?"

I shook my head. "Certainly not." I reached out for the basket and Persis grabbed up a stack of blankets and towels.

Outside there was no need for a lantern, for the flames leaping towards the sky made the scene as brilliant as a stage lit by red lamps. And the darting, shouting, shadowy figures made me think of illustrations I had seen in our school library, of Dante's Inferno.

We left the house and went down a path at the rear that led towards the fire. The heat was terrific, and the ugly crackling and sucking noise, made us shout to be heard.

We were both drenched with perspiration when Persis cried, "It's over this way."

We came up to a log cabin made of peeled logs, with a well in front, where a bucket brigade was working frantically. Here and there through the smoke I could see shirt-sleeved men throwing buckets of water, and directing the field hands in beating out the flames with blankets.

We entered the log house, where a very old black woman wearing a faded calico gown was standing in front of the fireplace.

"Honore has sent down some things, Molly," said Persis, "for you to doctor the hands. She said you would know what to do."

The old woman nodded and hobbled forward to examine the basket I had placed on the table. I was uncomfortable there, but Persis seemed unaffected. She began to roll up her sleeves.

"We'll help," she said. "You'll be needing some clean water, Molly."

"Yes, mistress."

Persis went to the door and called out. "One of you fetch a bucket of water in here quickly. And tell any of the hands with bad burns to come to Molly."

A man answered, and in a moment a young Negro carried in two huge buckets of water as easily as if they had been filled with feathers. I could see that his bare chest and shoulders were burned raw in places, but when Persis tried to make him wait for treatment he demurred, saying in his soft guttural voice. "Later, mistress. They's worse ones," as he ducked out.

The "worse" ones began to arrive at once, some staggering along by themselves, nearly overcome by the heat and smoke they had been working in, and others carried by their comrades.

I was appalled by their dreadful burns and touched by their stoicism and the depth of gratitude that shone in the black eyes as Persis and I, under Molly's direction, cleaned and bandaged their injuries.

One old man told Persis that the master had gotten the horses out, and had gone back to try and free the rest of the livestock. He didn't know whether or not they could save the stables.

After that I lost track of time. After what seemed hours of unceasing, backbreaking work, I was startled to hear a familiar voice at the door.

"Well, this is a sight I never expected to see, the Mistress of Harlequin working in the slave quarters."

I glanced up to see Clive Valerian's smoke blackened face, wearing its characteristic Mephistophelian smile. "Madame, I salute you."

He made a mock bow, and I could see his front hair had been singed and his clothes were in tatters, as if he had run through the brush. There was a long, livid burn like a brand across his cheek.

"What are you doing here?" I asked coldly.

"That is no way to greet a neighbor who has come at risk of life and limb—not to mention reputation—to offer help in your hour of need. In fact, a good samaritan, ma'am."

Nettled, I said, "My husband would not welcome finding you on his property, Mr. Valerian."

"Nor would I welcome finding him on mine. But this is an emergency. It is regretful that now and then Breckenridge and I have been forced to fight on the same side. It doesn't lessen our contempt for each other I assure you. I came mainly to save the horses. You know I am a lover of good horseflesh— about all there is left to admire in this new world of ours."

More to shut him up than anything else, I said, "You can be treated up at the house, by Honore."

"Ah, but I would not dream of stepping inside Harlequin House, Mrs. Rawlins. And your husband, if he knew, would think my treatment here quite appropriate. A very narrow-minded, stiff necked man, your husband. Blind, too. He only sees what he wants to see." There was a strange bitterness in his tone. "Besides, he is taking up all Honore's attention at the moment. Seton and I just pulled him out of the barn before it collapsed, and carried him up to the house."

Persis cried out behind me, and I felt my own heart give a sudden sickening lurch, due to guilt no doubt. Up in Harlequin Room, when I threw his love back in his face, I could have done it in a less blatant fashion.

Both Valerian and Persis were watching me closely.

"Well," said Persis, "aren't you going to him?"

"Yes," I stammered, "yes, of course."

"I'll stay here then." She turned back to her tasks. She was really a remarkable young lady I thought, and I wondered if Seton could be lingering nearby and would come to help her.

Clive Valerian insisted on walking me back to the house, and though he talked a great deal in his light insolent drawl, I barely took in a word he said.

At the back door he stopped me and said, "Please tell your husband that Seton and I are driving the horses to Marchmount, where we will stable them till he can send for them. They're much too valuable to be running loose, and we're the nearest place with stable room. And may I say again, you've surprised me tonight, Mrs. Rawlins."

On impulse I said, "Before all this

started, I had been planning a ball. I told my husband I intended to invite you and your family."

"How extraordinary. And what did he say?"

"Social matters are in my hands, Mr Valerian. Tell me, would you have accepted?"

He gave me a long, speculative look. "No, I wouldn't have—then."

"And now?"

"Let me say this: do you know your husband and I fought a duel?"

"Yes," I said. "He told me all about it."

"Indeed? His version. Someday I might tell you mine."

"Is that why you hate him so much—because he fought you, injured you?"

His voice grew harsh. "No, I hate him for his abysmal blindness and smugness, and because he didn't have the guts to finish what he started!"

I sighed. "Then it was useless; you never would have accepted my invitation?"

"Send it and see."

"But now—"

"Oh, you'll have to give your ball, Mrs. Rawlins. No matter what happens tonight, Breckenridge will insist upon it. Harlequin is going to need its ball after this—its one last brave gesture of indestructability."

I heard him laugh unpleasantly as he turned away.

There was no one in the kitchen when I

entered except one young frightened maid keeping the stove going. When I asked after her master, she told me he had been carried to his room.

I lifted my skirts, torn and stained now, and ran across the great hall and up the stairs. I found Aunt Samantha in the upstairs hall, dressed as if for the road even to her hat and gloves.

"My dear," she gasped, "I got ready in case we have to flee. I've never been through such a night in my life, not even during the war. Oh, do forgive me for mentioning it. And my poor heart—"

"Where is my husband?" I demanded, cutting off her chatter.

"Poor, dear, Breckenridge! They've taken him into his room. Honore is with him. It was a miracle someone pulled him out of the barn before—"

I left her abruptly and went to throw open the door to Breckenridge's room, not bothering to knock. At a glance I saw that his suite was a duplicate of my own.

He lay on his bed still partially dressed in his smoke-blackened clothes, with Honore bending over him. She had removed his shirt and I could see the livid burns across his chest and on his arms and hands.

He lay with his eyes closed, but at the sound of my voice asking how he was, he opened them and said, "I'm fine, my dear wife. Honore can do all that needs to be done. You might ask Forbes to report to me as soon as he can."

"Yes, of course," I said, subdued and slightly angered by his rude tone.

"You could say," he added with a sardonic twist of his lips, "that this has been a fatal day for both Harlequin and its master. A day of irreparable—losses."

As I turned away he started to laugh, but I heard him catch his breath and it ended in a stifled groan.

I went back downstairs and out the front door, stopping the first man I met to ask him to find Forbes and send him to the house. Then I sat quietly in the hall waiting, with my thoughts in a turmoil and such a welter of conflicting emotions, that despite my efforts to control it I began to weep. Like a child in a disaster, frightened, bewildered, I wept without understanding exactly why.

13

Harlequin seemed very strange for the next few days, quiet and withdrawn, like an injured beast licking its wounds. The fire had been controlled that first night, and then fully extinguished the next day, but my husband kept to his room, receiving only Sam Forbes. The rest of us talked in subdued tones and ate mostly silent meals, trying to avoid each other's eyes.

Outside, the lush green fields had been blackened as if by some hideous blight. The barn and some of the stables had fallen in, and many of the outbuildings lay in charred ruins. It was a sickening and a disheartening sight.

I had not seen Breckenridge since the night of the fire, when I entered his bedroom, and he had turned me out coldly. I couldn't blame him really, and there seemed nothing for me to do but leave as I had told him was my intention. On the other hand, my own sense of pride and responsibility would not let me go while the plantation was in such chaos, and its master lay ill and helpless.

I was left to my own resources, for Aunt Samantha was prostrate with a delayed nervous reaction, Honore was busy attending to her master. Persis continued working with old Molly, getting the farm hands back into shelters of some kind, and declined my help. I spent a good deal of time reading in my room, or writing letters. Much as I longed to, I did not write to John, as I did not think it yet proper, but I wrote the Campbells I would be visiting them soon. I was just finishing the letter, having added the hasty postscript that when I came, I hoped to see John again so that I might give him my condolences, when someone knocked at the door.

"Come in," I called, and was surprised to see Breckenridge step into the room, closing the door behind him. His hands were still bandaged as, I presumed, were his chest and shoulders, for he stood a little stiffly in his gray coat, his face pale under its dark skin.

"I'm sorry to trouble you," he said, "but I felt we should have a short talk."

"Of course," I replied, "won't you sit down?"

He took a seat a bit awkwardly, on a chair facing me, and clasped his bandaged hands between his knees.

"I'm very sorry about Harlequin," I said, "and—for your own injuries."

"Thank you, but they don't amount to anything. Honore is an excellent nurse."

"Can you save anything of the crops?" I asked.

His eyes were on the carpet and not a muscle moved in his face. "No," he said flatly.

"How dreadful. But at least the horses are all safe at Marchmount?"

His lips tightened in a bitter line. "Yes. But I wish they were anywhere else."

"There was nowhere else to send them that night, and both Seton and Mr. Valerian worked very hard."

"And pulled me out of the burning barn too, I am told. Quite the heroes."

"They saved your life," I said sharply.

"I want no favors from the Valerians! They'd done better to let me stay where I was."

"How can you be so cold and ungrateful! You may consider them your enemies, but they acted that night as friends."

"And now they have secured a champion in our midst?"

"Yes!" I cried, annoyed. "I, at least, give credit where credit is due, and I am grateful for what they did that dreadful night."

"Are you, my dear wife?" He seemed faintly amused, which infuriated me still more. I opened my mouth to continue, but he made a quick gesture with one of his bandaged hands and silenced me.

"I really came to discuss something quite apart from the fire," he told me. "I wanted to ask if you still intend to leave Harlequin at once, or if you would remain to act as hostess for the Harlequin ball on the first of next month. That will give us time I believe, to get at least the house in order."

I stared at him in amazement. "But you can't be thinking of going ahead with a ball now?"

His jaw hardened. "Why not?"

"But—everything at Harlequin is in ruins!"

"I beg to differ with you," he said sharply. "Harlequin House has not been touched. It is just as it has always been."

And I recalled Clive Valerian's words to me the night of the fire. "You'll have to give your ball, Mrs. Rawlins. No matter what happens tonight, Breckenridge will insist upon it. Harlequin is going to need its ball after this—its one last gesture of indestructability."

I saw him studying me with that same watchful concentration he had shown when he first talked to me at Judge Campbell's house about our marriage.

"Will you do this one last thing?" he asked.

I threw out my hands in a helpless gesture. "I suppose so, but it all seems so foolish, so futile."

"Will you kindly let me decide what is

foolish or futile for Harlequin?" He sounded weary and there were beads of perspiration on his forehead and upper lip; it had no doubt been a difficult conversation for him. He said in a more conciliatory tone, "Honore and Aunt Samantha will help you."

He got to his feet with that same stiff, awkward motion I had noted when he sat down. "Thank you. After the ball—well, you will be free to leave."

I opened my mouth to say something more, to offer some word of sympathy perhaps, but he turned on his heel abruptly and left the room. I realized that Breckenridge and I were poles apart now, and surely this was what I had wanted—yet I was aware of a certain depression. Then something else claimed my attention. The letter I had just finished to Mrs. Campbell, with its hastily scrawled postscript, had lain all this while on the little table between our chairs, and I recalled that Breckenridge had sat for a long time with his eyes downcast. Undoubtedly he had been unable to avoid reading it. My cheeks grew hot at the memory. On impulse I snatched up the letter and tore it to shreds, not knowing quite why I did so.

I retired early that night. It was unusually hot and humid, and I awoke around midnight quite suddenly, with every faculty alert. Something besides the night birds had disturbed me.

I lay quietly inside the mosquito netting, and abruptly I knew what it was. The shadow, or whatever it was, of that ancient Harlequin bride was moving again in my dressing room. I now always kept the door tightly shut at night, but I could distinctly hear the rustle of cloth over the floor boards.

This time, I resolved grimly, I was going to *see* this thing, whether apparition or human. I crept out of bed on bare feet, as silently as possible, threw a silk wrapper around me, and inched towards the door. There was bright moonlight coming in through the shuttered windows. There were no windows, of course, in the dressing room and no light came from under the bedroom door. I lit a candle and, shielding its flame with my hand, went to the dressing room door. The knob only made the slightest of sounds, as I drew the door open hastily and thrust my hand, holding the candle, inside.

Nothing.

There was nothing to see, just the blank cupboard wall, the dressing table, and the cloudy mirror above.

I felt anger rise in me, for I was certain I was being tricked somehow. I put the candle down close to the floor and examined it minutely. There wasn't a mark, a scrap of dust, or so much as a thread. I got up and turned to the cupboards. Someone, or something, I was sure, had access to the dressing room.

I started at one end and deliberately emptied every drawer and closet. I could find nothing odd or out of the way. I concentrated

at last on the largest of the rather shallow
closets. This one was a bit wider than the
others. When it was empty I stepped inside. I
pressed and prodded each section of pan-
eling, but nothing gave or seemed loose. I
bent to examine the four inch baseboard
that circled the little space. As I did so, the
edge of my wrapper caught on one of the
roughened corners. I tugged at it irritably,
made impatient by frustration and defeat.
Suddenly that portion of the baseboard
lifted a fraction of an inch. I stooped at once
and got my fingers underneath it. More of it
lifted. Then, getting both hands under the
section, I raised it about four inches. Against
the boards beneath was a small knob. I
pressed it with trembling fingers, and the
rear panel swung open. I pushed the opening
wider, picked up my candle, and stepped
inside.

It was a narrow corridor, evidently built
between the thick stone walls. There was a
heavy layer of dust along the floor except in
the center, where it looked as if some sort of
cloth or rag had been dragged.

I felt so elated that I kept on even
though mice scurried around and even over
my bare feet. Phantom bride indeed, I
thought! Someone in this house had simply
been trying to frighten me. But why? To
make me leave? But it didn't make sense. I
was an asset to the Rawlins household, and
now, after the destruction by the fire, they
would need my help more than ever. The

servants? But they were loyal to the Rawlinses and to Harlequin House. What would they have to gain by chasing me away? One thought sobered me—the fact that if I died as Breckenridge's wife, he would inherit my fortune as next of kin. Regardless of the distrubing thought, I went forward accompanied by the eerie shadows and the close, dusty air. I had to know what lay behind all this.

I had begun to climb shallow steps. I went up and up, the narrow passage twisting and turning like the coils of a serpent. I began to wonder if my candle would last out the climb. Whoever had come this way to my dressing room must have come from a very great distance. Then suddenly I was in a tiny, box-like room. There was a door at one end set into a very low stone arch. I put my hand on the latch and inched it open. It made no sound. Someone, I thought grimly, had carefully oiled the ancient hinges. There was something thick and heavy shrouding the entrance. I put out my hand and touched what appeared to be dusty canvas.

Then I stopped like an animal frozen in its tracks.

Two voices came from the other side, partially muffled by the canvas wall or whatever it was, but unmistakably that of a man and a woman.

The woman was laughing softly, and I held my breath to try to catch her words.

"But darling, what are you worried

about? It's all been so absurdly simple. I tell you she doesn't suspect a thing."

The man's voice was lower, less distinct, or perhaps he was farther away.

"—take chances, it's so near the end now."

"It's all going exactly as planned. I declare, sometimes I wonder why I love you. There are those who would say I was a fool. Am I a fool, my dearest?"

I heard the man's voice say something very softly in reply, but I couldn't decipher the words.

The woman spoke more loudly a moment later. "I still don't understand why you think this silly ball is the time to—"

"Be still!" he whispered fiercely. "I warned you not to talk about it—even when we're alone!"

"All right, darling," she drawled carelessly, and suddenly I knew who she was.

Rina.

Rina Vinton!

And in a flash I knew where I was. On the other side of the tapestry, in what had been the priest's hole in the Harlequin Room! But what did it all mean? Who was the man in there with Rina? And how had they gotten a key to the room?

I put my candle on one of the steps leading down from the tiny room, where it would show no glimmer, and went back to carefully pull aside one corner of the tapestry. Dust shook down even at the slight movement,, and I was afraid I would sneeze, but I managed to stifle the need. Now that I had a few inches of view into the Harlequin Room, I could make out two shadowy figures standing close together near the little altar.

Only a feeble light, cast no doubt by their own candle which probably rested on the same table by the door where Breckenridge had placed his, outlined their forms. I could see Rina was wearing a very full old-fashioned skirt—the dragging cloth I had heard in the dressing room, no doubt. The man was more in shadow facing away from the light, but suddenly he put his arms around Rina and drew her towards him, and I could see the white bandages on his hands as they touched her back and shoulders.

It was Breckenridge in there, making love to Rina where he pretended to make love to me.

I let the tapestry drop from my fingers, aware of a sudden numbing coldness that I had never felt before. I was sure of only one thing: I had to get back to my own room somehow, without their hearing me. And I had to get out of this terrible house as quickly as possible.

I don't even recall going back down the passageway and into my now doubly hateful dressing room, but somehow I must have done so, putting everything back in its place, for the next morning the room looked just as usual when Honore came to help me to dress.

As she was doing my hair she glanced sharply at my face. "Madame does not feel well?"

"I'm quite all right, Honore," I said.

"But you perhaps did not sleep well? The heat?"

I nodded. "Yes, I was a bit restless."

"Then tonight you must take a sleeping draught, like the one I have given each night to the master since his injury."

I smiled grimly, thinking that if she had given Breckenridge a draught last night he had probably poured it out the window before going to join Rina.

I knew that I would have to see him once more before I packed, to tell him that I had changed my mind and was leaving Harlequin at once. Whatever he and Rina had planned for the night of his precious ball would never come off. But neither would I give him the satisfaction of just leaving him a note to be read after my departure, and have him think I had run away simply out of fear of him.

"How is Aunt Samantha?" I asked, to change the subject.

"Oh, madame, she improves hourly since the announcement of the ball to be held next month. Such a change you would not have believed." Honore gave me one of her rare smiles. "You have brought us all hope and pleasure again at Harlequin since you came, madame."

I thought that their pleasure would be

short-lived indeed, and felt a pang of regret for Aunt Samantha and Persis and Honore, but I knew that nothing would stop me from leaving the place now.

"Is Mr. Rawlins at home?" I asked. "I must speak to him."

"I regret, madame, he left at dawn with Forbes, to go to the bank at Croix. He asked me to tell you that he would not return until late tonight."

"Thank you." I did not want Honore to know of my plans until I was ready to execute them. I could pack myself, and be ready to leave the house tonight, at whatever time Breckenridge returned. I was determined not to wait longer.

I found Samantha and Persis, seated at the breakfast table, feverishly working on guest lists and menus. I hadn't the heart to disillusion them, especially when Persis leaped up and gave me an impulsive kiss, saying, "Tamson, you are the only one who could have gotten Cousin Breckenridge to give the ball after all! It's going to be the most wonderful event of my life!" She went whirling off to the drawing room, and a moment later we could hear her playing a spirited polka.

"That child has never been so excited in her life," sighed Aunt Samantha happily. "You have been so good for Harlequin, Tamson—and for all of us. We owe you so much."

There were tears in her eyes which I

simply couldn't face, so I patted her hand and wandered out onto the terrace. There was still a trace of scorched earth smell, but everywhere I could see men working happily to restore order. I wondered what Breckenridge's little scheme with Rina could be. Well, it would not affect me, for I would be gone long before his precious ball.

But I could not anticipate the trick that Harlequin House would play to insure getting its own way.

14

After dinner I sat alone in my room, having directed Honore to inform me the minute my husband returned.

At last, feeling unusually hot, I lay down fully dressed and closed my eyes for what seemed only a moment. When I awoke sometime later, I was aware of a mounting fever. Chills ran up and down my spine and made my teeth chatter. Somehow I managed to drag myself out of bed and ring for Honore, I remember little more, for when she arrived Honore found me lying by the bell-pull.

I have only a faint recollection of the days and weeks that followed my attack of malaria. I was dimly aware of faces, voices, people hovering over me, of being forced to drink liquids and of alternating between blazing fever and icy chills that seemed to dissolve my bones.

When at last I opened my eyes one morning as Honore bent over me, and knew her face and where I was, I felt almost too spent to speak.

"How long have I been ill?" I whispered, aware of my dry cracked lips.

"Oh, madame, thank the good Lord you have come to your senses at last! It has been almost three weeks that you have lain here."

"Three—weeks?"

"Yes, but you will mend quickly now. I know this malaria—here, drink this." And she gently raised me up until I had drained the glass she held to my lips. "Now, sleep, madame. By nightfall you will be much improved."

I was astonished to find that this was true. When I awoke at dusk, I was stronger, even a little hungry. Honore stayed with me until I had eaten most of the chicken soup she brought me, and washed me and arranged my hair in fresh plaits and helped me into a frilly pink bed jacket.

"The master has been waiting impatiently to see you," she said.

"But I can't see him now—I—"

She paid no attention to me as she gathered up the dishes and went to the door.

A moment later Breckenridge stepped into the room and came to the bed swiftly, his eyes studying my face with a strange anxiety. Honore had left the netting pushed back, and he reached forward to grasp my hand.

"Tamson—how are you feeling?"

"Better," I said as lightly as I could. I did not want him holding my hand, and I gently withdrew it to touch my hair.

"We've—all been so worried about you. I'm convinced you over-taxed your strength the night of the fire. You should not have tried to do so much."

"I did no more than Persis."

"But you are not used to our climate. Our summers are extremely enervating. If I had been aware of it I would have prevented your going to the servants' quarters."

"It's over and done with," I said shortly.

A shadow crossed his face, but he forced a smile and said, "Now better times are coming. The ball is to be held in ten days. We have everything in readiness, the new furnishings have arrived from New Orleans, and Honore tells me you will be well enough by then to take your place as the hostess of Harlequin. I—I have a great surprise for you also."

I knew that this was the moment to tell him I would not be attending the ball under any circumstances, but as usual he gave me no chance. He took my hand again and pressed it to his lips quickly and gently, and was out of the room before I could speak.

I did not see him in the days that followed, and I was amazed at how rapidly my strength and vigor returned. I had an enormous appetite, and ate everything Honore brought me. She laughed, delighted at my complete recovery, and told me that this was often the way with malaria patients.

Samantha and Persis were in and out of my room at all hours, showing me the huge response to the written invitations, displaying their new ball gowns and hairdos, and telling me in constant wonder that Breckenridge had made no protest when they timidly told him that the Valerians had elected to come.

I decided at last that for Persis' and Aunt Samantha's sakes I might as well stay for the ball, and leave directly afterwards. It would cause less talk, and I felt sorry for the two happy women. I suddenly found myself, perhaps with the detachment of a long illness, not caring what Rina and Breckenridge had planned for the night of the ball.

Rina had not been to see me during my illness, but when I went downstairs a few mornings later to try my legs, I was surprised to learn that she had left Harlequin on the night I fell ill, and had gone to Charleston to visit friends.

"You mean she won't be here for the ball?" I asked Aunt Samantha.

"Well, I'm sure she will, dear. But Rina has always been so very independent, not really like a southern gentlewoman in some respects." She blushed, adding, "I didn't mean that she's not a lady."

I smiled at her. "Of course not. I'm just surprised she left so suddenly."

Persis, coming in the door, tossed her

pretty head and said, "Oh, I think she left because she and Cousin Breckenridge had words. At least she went to see him in his study the night you were taken ill, and then she packed and left. And good riddance I think; she's so stuck up."

"Persis!" cried Aunt Samantha.

"Well, it's true. I never did like her or her sister, Anabelle. They were both alike."

"Persis, dear, it is not seemly to speak ill of the dead, and Breckenridge was so devoted to her."

But Persis merely flounced off not looking in the least repentant.

I was amused by her, but I wondered what double game this was, that Rina and Breckenridge were playing at now. I had heard her say that she loved him, and I had seen him embrace her in the Harlequin Room. I felt uneasy in the great house, as if some unseen danger stalked me, and I decided to write Mrs. Campbell at once that I would be coming to Boston as quickly as possible.

When I went for a stroll in the garden a little later, I was surprised to find Persis seemingly lurking behind a lilac bush.

"Please," she said softly, "may I speak to you for a moment?"

"Of course," I said in surprise.

She glanced quickly up at the house before she went on. "I don't want anyone to overhear us."

"Is something wrong, Persis?"

"It's Cousin Breckenridge, really. He listens to you. I know if you spoke to him—"

I was wryly amused at her faith in my power to sway Breckenridge, but I said, "Tell me what's the matter."

"I—well, the night of the fire, after you came back to the house with Clive Valerian, Seton came into the cabin to help me. He worked very hard; he stayed until morning. I—well, I don't think I ever really knew what he was like. You know how Breckenridge feels about the Valerians—and how Clive feels about us?"

"Yes," I said, still puzzled.

I saw Persis lick her lips and then she blurted out, "Seton and I have been meeting each other ever since, down by the river—we love each other. You've got to help us, Tamson!"

I was taken off guard by her words and yet really not surprised; from the beginning they had somehow seemed meant for each other.

"You don't think we've been terrible, Tamson? There's never been anything really—wrong between us."

"Of course I don't think it's terrible," I told her. "You are both young of course, and there are obstacles, but I think you should be allowed to see each other openly."

She threw her arms around me impulsively, her eyes shining with joy. "Oh, I knew you would understand and help us!"

"I may understand," I said, "but I'm not

sure just how I can help you."

"But if you speak to Cousin Breckenridge—"

I said kindly, "I can't promise anything, Persis, but I will discuss this with Breckenridge, and try to make him understand."

"Oh, thank you, thank you! You are the very best thing that ever happened to Harlequin House!"

As she raced off, no doubt to meet Seton somewhere, I reflected bitterly that Harlequin House was the worst thing that could have happened to *me*. If I had never met Breckenridge Rawlin, or heard of Harlequin House, I might have remained in Boston and be waiting there now, free, to greet John Markham.

15

The day of the ball dawned fairly overcast,
but by the time the first breeze of afternoon
had come, the sky was a faultless blue, and
Honore informed me that there would be
stars and a full moon.

I went downstairs with Persis to inspect
the great ballroom and found it transformed
into a bower of fragrant blossoms—lilacs,
roses, hyacinths, garlands of honeysuckle
and jasmine, and great waxy magnolias. A
Haitian orchestra had been hired in Charleston, Persis told me proudly, and would play
from the old minstrels' gallery now made
gay with flags and bunting. Supper was to be
an enormous buffet with three huge tables
for the food, and twenty-five servants in
uniforms to serve. Everyone, simply everyone in the countryside, said Persis, eyes
sparkling, was coming to Harlequin that
night.

I wondered about Rina Vinton. Did she intend to come openly, brazenly, or in secret, down the passage from the Harlequin Room so that she and Breckenridge would put their little plan, whatever it was, into action? If so, they were in for a surprise.

Several days before, I had asked one of the male servants to fit bolts to all the closet doors in my dressing room. I had asked him not to mention this to anyone, and had given him a sizable tip to insure his silence.

The night of the ball, as I completed my toilet in the dressing room, I felt secure for the first time. Although she noticed the new bolts, Honore made no mention of them to me as she helped me into my rose satin and tulle ball gown, with its tiny stars of bugle beads edging the scallops of the skirt.

I wore the Yorke amethysts at my throat, but shook my head when Honore offered me the amethyst ring Breckenridge had given me. I still looked a trifle drawn and pale from my illness, but my shoulders were creamy above the deep decollete of the gown, and my arms firmly rounded above my long white gloves.

Outside my window I could hear the rattle of carriage wheels, and the exchange of gay voices as the guests began to arrive. Honore told me that Aunt Samantha and Persis were already downstairs in the reception hall, and I knew that I must hurry to join them, but as I rose and picked up my fan a knock sounded at the door.

Honore opened it and my husband strolled in. He was immaculate in faultless evening clothes, and his dark eyes held that same intense watchful light I had seen in them the first time we met. He stood looking at me until Honore left the room.

"You look very beautiful, Mrs. Rawlins," he said lightly. "I suppose you do not object to bearing that title for the last time to-night?"

I inclined my head.

He reached into an inside coat pocket and brought out an envelope. "Before we go down to greet our guests, I would like you to have this. Please open it."

I took it from him, fumbling a bit with the flap because of my gloves, before I got it open. I stared in surprise at its contents. It was a bank draft made out to me for the full amount I had advanced him on our marriage.

I glanced up at him inquiringly. "But I don't understand—surely the fire wiped out all your funds? I told you there was no immediate need to repay me."

"There was and is an immediate need," he answered sharply. "You are leaving, aren't you, after the ball?" Again there was that disturbing speculative look in his eyes.

"Yes," I said, "that is my intention."

"Then I couldn't let you leave Harlequin without ending our—bargain honorably.

"But I don't see how you raised the money?"

"That is my own damned business!" he exploded. "Are you ready to go down?"

"Yes!" I retorted just as hotly. There was really no use in speaking to the man, he was intolerable. And I had meant to use these moments alone with him to discuss Persis and Seton, but I knew he would listen to nothing on the subject now.

He gave me his arm which I took with distaste, and we descended the stairs in an icy silence.

It seemed to me that the huge hall below was filled to overflowing with women in lavish gowns and jewels, and men of all ages wearing faultless evening attire.

Aunt Samantha, looking distinguished in a gold moire gown, and Persis lovely as a young lily in white lace over panels of cream satin, with a wreath of tiny white roses in her fair hair, stood receiving the guests. Breckenridge and I went to join them.

At my husband's side, the faces became a blur to me as we stood for what seemed hours, welcoming our guests. But at last it was over and we could join them in the ballroom. Gilt chairs and benches had been placed against the wall and I longed to sit down on one of them and rest. But Aunt Samantha whispered to Breckenridge that we must start the ball by having the first dance.

She signaled the orchestra with her fan, and they began to play The Emperor Waltz. Breckenridge took me lightly in his arms

and we moved out upon the polished floor—
that same floor that had felt the feet of so
many dancers down through the centuries—
and as we slowly circled I had a giddy sense
of unreality. Breckenridge was an excellent
dancer, and I seemed to float back to the
door as the other couples moved out to join
us.

Aunt Samantha pressed a dance pro-
gram into my hands saying, "My dear, every
man here wants to dance with you!"

And I did dance with what seemed to me
every man in the room. Most of them were
strangers, of course, except Virgil Jessup
and Pierre Legros, who had come from
Croix.

Pierre Legros was very gallant. "You
look most beautiful, madame. You grace this
room like a star, and I see there are stars on
your gown. You have made Harlequin and
my good friend, Breckenridge, very happy.
And you, madame, are you not happy here
in this ancient and amiable house?"

I lied prettily and told him I was very
happy. Since he seemed to believe me I
realized I must be a very convincing actress.

Seton and Persis danced by, seemingly
lost in a world of their own. I glanced around
to see if Breckenridge was watching them,
but I could not see him anywhere. I had not
yet seen Rina Vinton at the ball and I
wondered if they could be somewhere together.

I danced with Seton, and he said at

once, "You've been wonderful to Persis and me, Mrs. Rawlins. I realize Breckenridge doesn't approve of my attentions to Persis, and for that matter neither does Clive. It's a pity, and all so senseless. Our families used to be friends, you know."

"You and Persis," I said, "mustn't pay any attention to the feud or whatever it is. Of course it's senseless, but perhaps time will remedy that."

"I hope so," he sighed.

"Where is your brother?" I asked curiously.

"At the bar most likely," Seton answered, with a wry twist of his lips. "I only hope he won't cause any sort of trouble tonight. Mrs. Rawlins, you were most generous to invite us. If the invitation had come from anyone else in this house, I'm sure Clive would have refused it. Here he comes now."

Clive's tall figure came across the room towards us, and though his gait was steady enough, it was plain from his bright eyes and flushed face that he had been drinking a good deal. He bowed to me and gravely requested the pleasure of the next dance. I took his arm and was grateful that it was a measured waltz. Surprisingly Clive Valerian was an excellent and effortless dancer, even better than Breckenridge.

He said, giving me that strange twisted smile of his, "I do congratulate you, Mrs. Rawlins."

"Congratulate me, Mr. Valerian?"

"For bringing all this off, for showing them what Yankee stubbornness and dollars can do. Why you've even produced the Valerians *en masse*, and minding their best manners."

I said stiffly, "My husband is giving the ball, as you well know."

"But it is for your sake. He wants you to see Harlequin as it was, the fool! Nothing here in the South can ever be as it was; I know that, and so does every other man in the room but stiff-necked Breckenridge Rawlins!"

People were staring at us as Clive's voice had risen. I didn't want a scene, but I stopped dancing. "Please, Mr. Valerian, you are forgetting yourself."

He had the grace to flush and he said quickly, "Your pardon, madame. I seem to have taken a glass too many. Will you walk in the garden with me—or are you afraid to?"

"Why should I be afraid? Of course I will." I led the way out to the terrace and at once the cooler air seemed to bring my companion to his senses. He asked me if he might light a cigar, and when I gave my permission we strolled slowly down the path between the hedges.

"You have a kind heart," he said after a time, in a perfectly sober voice. "It's not a usual thing to find in a woman."

"Perhaps you have known the wrong kind of women, Mr. Valerian. There is a great deal more kindness in people than you might think."

He laughed. "That, my dear lady, is a girlish dream—as even Breckenridge could tell you. You are not very worldly."

"I suppose not; I've led a sheltered life up to now. Is there so much advantage to being worldly?"

"Not for you," he said quietly, then added, "I should hate to see you lose your faith in the things that count, become cynical like me—and Breckenridge."

"You think my husband is cynical?"

"Don't you? Bitter at least."

"In some ways perhaps. But he still believes in some things. He believes in Harlequin."

He threw away his cigar impatiently. "That's his damned, beg pardon, stubborn pride! He never could see the truth of anything. The night of the fire you said Breckenridge had told you about our duel?"

I nodded.

"And I said it was his version, and someday I would tell you mine. Would you care to hear it now?"

I took a deep breath. I wasn't sure I wanted to know anything more about that duel fought so long ago, a painful episode that seemed to have affected all our lives. But Clive Valerian was watching me curiously, quite obviously expecting me to refuse, so I said, "Of course."

He led me to a stone bench and we sat

down. He lowered his head and let his hands dangle between his spread knees.

"You know about the Vintons, Rina and—Anabelle?"

"Yes."

"Before the war Rina was still a child, but Anabelle was a lovely and high spirited young woman. She spent a good deal of time here at Harlequin, and both Breckenridge and I courted her after a fashion. She liked to play us against each other, but that was all part of the game. Breckenridge put her on a pedestal and treated her like some kind of saint. I understood her true nature better and treated her like a woman. She actually preferred me for it, and I felt that I was falling in love with her. I was no idealist even then, but I thought that once she enjoyed her frivolity and flirting like any young girl, she would settle down into decent womanhood.

"She adored the life and glitter of Charleston, and I often accompanied her there where she stayed with friends." He raised his head. "I had no way of knowing how she occupied her time while I was not with her. One day I proposed and she accepted like a shot. I was surprised, because knowing Anabelle, I did not think she was ready yet to give up her gay life for one man. I hadn't spoken to her family yet, so we kept the news of the engagement a secret during the remainder of our stay in Charleston. Then one afternoon I met a friend in the

Jockey Club—he told me of the sailor she had been seen with after dark down by the dockside two months back. I was no more than amused at first because I knew about her flirtations, all perfectly harmless I thought. But that night when I mentioned it to chide her, she flew into a rage, and then the whole sordid story came out. She had loved him and he had betrayed her. He had told her he was going to carry her off to England with him, and she had believed him. She was carrying his child, but she gave me to understand that, as a gentleman, she was going to hold me to my promise of marriage. I told her quite frankly that though I would keep her secret for as long as she wished, I had no intentions of marrying her. I left her there in Charleston, and when I heard she was back at Harlequin, I stayed away.

"She let out hints, of course, that she was in love with me and that I had asked her to marry me and then gone back on my word. I couldn't ·refuse her openly, but I stayed out of reach. She preyed on the Rawlinses sympathies, and I don't doubt she had a try at marrying Breckenridge. But she must have lost heart or grown desperate, or perhaps she thought it the best way to punish me, for she drowned herself in the river and left a note accusing me of her downfall and of failing to live up to my word. It was useless by then for me to tell the truth, or my side of it. I would only make matters worse and label myself more of a cad than I already was in everyone's eyes."

"But surely someone would have believed you?"

He gave me a sad look. "In the South, that hot-bed of unswerving gallantry—who would believe it of a woman like Anabelle, with distant Rawlins connections, an honored guest at Harlequin House?"

"But your friend—the man who told you about the sailor?"

"He wouldn't utter publicly against a lady, even to save my already spotty reputation. No, there was nothing to be done, but hope that in time people's memories would grow a bit dimmer. They don't, though, you know, not about the bad things in one's life. No, my dear Tamson, if I may presume to call you that in the dark of this garden, you will have to learn that life is real, life is earnest."

"But it's all so unfair! Surely someone else must know the truth?"

"Perhaps, whoever they are they are determined never to speak up."

I said with sudden horror, "But you and Breckenridge could have been killed because of it!"

His smile was not nice to see; it reminded me of the bared fangs of a wolf. "That's right. Because even dead and disgraced, your husband would keep Anabelle on her pedestal, and insist on making himself the champion of the wronged woman. But even *that* he couldn't do like a man!" The words burst hotly from his lips.

"But surely you didn't expect him to shoot you down in cold blood, after honor had been satisfied?"

"He could have made a clean sweep of it—ended what he started! In his place that's what I would have done! But he wanted me to go on suffering the sting of disgrace for the rest of my life. I told you he's a blind stubborn fool. He doesn't deserve a wife like you, Tamson. I wouldn't blame you if you left him."

He glanced at me keenly and I felt myself blushing. He could not know how close he was to the truth, but nevertheless, I could not face his inquiring eyes. Clive Valerian was too intuitive by far, and I had no desire for him to know my secrets. "I think we'd better go," I said, rising. "I am the hostess after all. Thank you for telling me your side of the story."

"But you don't believe it?" he said sardonically as he got to his feet.

"I didn't say that. I have no way of knowing all the facts; I don't suppose anyone has now. But lacking absolute proof, my father always believed in giving a person the benefit of the doubt. I feel the same way. I don't think this—feud should go on, tainting everyone's lives. The past is over and done with, and there are others to consider. You and Breckenridge owe Harlequin and Marchmount your undivided attention now. The past must be buried."

"I think," mused Clive Valerian, "that with a woman like you beside me, I might be able to do that. If it were not already too late in my case." He added more kindly, "You don't, of course, understand our position here in the South. Oh, not the war, that's a segment in itself like a huge tidal wave, and its effects will go on forever, but it's our past generations we can't escape from. The old ways, the old mores, the deadly chivalry that binds us all as tightly as a steel chain. I've seen other southerners who have tried to break away, who have gone to the Indies, or Europe or out West, but they can't change what they are, what they'll always be."

"I think I understand," I said as we walked slowly back to the house. "You are indebted to the past in a way that most Americans are not?"

"Exactly; you do understand. I would never have believed it. But realizing that the hampering burden it represents, I can't see how a young woman of your beauty and intelligence and wealth came to marry Breckenridge. He won't change, you know. Or did love blind you to everything else?"

We had reached the steps of the terrace and I could see my husband just coming through the open door.

"Thank you for showing me the garden," I said, offering my hand to Clive Valerian. Bowing in return, he lifted my fingers to his lips briefly. "My great and honored pleasure, madame."

"There you are," said Breckenridge with a slight frown on his face. "I've been looking for you, Tamson."

"I'm coming," I replied lightly. "Mr. Valerian and I have just had a stroll about the garden. It's so warm inside."

Breckenridge said nothing but stood by the door waiting for me to join him before he offered me his arm and led me inside. Clive Valerian remained at the foot of the terrace steps, and I was glad that I had not had to think up a suitable reply to his last question.

Breckenridge did not ask me to dance as I had expected, but led me around the edge of the ballroom to the main door, where Aunt Samantha was still holding court.

"Oh, my dears, I have been looking for you," she began, but Breckenridge cut her off rather crisply.

"Later, Aunt Samantha. You hold the fort for awhile; Tamson and I have something important to attend to."

Looking a bit bewildered, Aunt Samantha said, "Well, if it's really important, dear—"

He didn't wait for her to finish but wheeled me out into the now empty great hall, and led me rapidly towards his study.

"I am a bit tired," I said, "and I do appreciate the respite, but you needn't have used the excuse that we have something important to do."

"But it's the truth. I want to show you

something," he answered shortly.

I glanced at his rigid profile as we hurried along, learning nothing from it. Was he angry because I had been outside alone in the garden with Clive Valerian? Or was all this part of the plan he and Rina had been discussing while I watched them in each other's arms in the Harlequin Room? I felt a desire to free myself from his arm but he gave me no chance.

Then he paused suddenly in front of the study door and released me. "You will find what I wanted to show you inside." He glanced briefly at my amethyst necklace and then down at my gloved hands. "I don't suppose you bothered to wear your ring?" His mouth twisted wryly and when I did not reply he added, "No, I hadn't expected it. We've always been at loggerheads, haven't we, Tamson? You seem to prefer anyone's company to mine, even Clive Valerian's. No matter, just this once I mean to give you something that will please you, something that will make your memory of me less— repugnant."

Could he know, I thought wildly, that I had seen and heard him with Rina in the Harlequin Room? But that was not possible.

"Go inside," he said suddenly, "go and see if you approve of my last gift to you, my dear."

He turned abruptly leaving me there startled and rather angry. He really was completely unpredictable and quite rude at times. I even thought darkly that this might be part of his plotting with Rina. I saw that he did not return towards the ballroom, nor did he glance back at me. Instead he took a cigar from his pocket and strolled out the front door nodding briefly to the two servants dressed in livery, who stood at attention on either side.

Out of the corner of their eyes I could feel them watching me. I had no intention of making a spectacle of myself before the servants, nor of providing them with tidbits for kitchen gossip. I reached out to grasp the handle of the study door firmly, thrust it open, and stepped inside.

Suddenly I felt as if some giant had dealt me a tremendous blow over the heart, and every drop of blood in my body seemed to drain away like water into sand. I took a faltering step forward with the room spinning around me, but for a split second my fading eyesight had registered the smiling face of John Markham.

16

When I came to I was lying on the sofa in front of the fireplace, and John Markham was chaffing my wrists and gazing down into my face anxiously, while Honore wafted a bottle of smelling salts under my nose. I pushed Honore's hand away. So it hadn't been a dream, a wild figment of my imagination, I thought; John was really here in the room with me.

I cried out, still unable to believe it.

"Tamson!" There was relief and joy in John's voice. "Are you all right?"

"Perfectly," I laughed, and sat up with his arm to support me. I convinced Honore that I was completely recovered, and sent her away. Then I turned to John. "I can't believe I'm really seeing you, John. How did you get here?" And then I remembered Breckenridge's telling me about the surprise he had for me. He had known, of course, that

223

John was in this room waiting for me. He must have arranged it! But I was too puzzled and too elated to dissect the puzzle further.

John sat beside me keeping my hand in his almost absently, like a child will grasp the hand of a parent.

"Breckenridge sent me a letter, Tamson," he began awkwardly. "He said you were to know nothing about it. He—told me a great many things. He invited me to come here as his guest. He is quite a gentleman, really."

I couldn't have cared less why he was here, or what Breckenridge's reasons were for sending for him. I could not take my gaze from his face, noting the new lines there but seeing also that he looked fully recovered from his wound.

"Tell me," I commanded, "everything that happened and about—Lucy, if you can? I can't tell you how sorry I am, John."

He bowed his head for a moment and I thought he was not going to discuss the subject, perhaps couldn't, and then I heard his voice low and dragging. But after that first painful hesitation, the words seemed to pour out in a torrent as if a dam had been broken.

It was a dreadful story, a young bride and groom, so much in love and so confident of their future in a wild new land. And then the sudden Indian attack that had taken them by surprise and cut their column in half, murdering most of them in cold blood before help could come.

John's cheeks and my own were wet when he finished, and all I could think to do to comfort him was to press his hands in mine and murmur, "John, poor dearest, John!"

"I had to leave her out there," he said in an anguished voice, "buried in a simple Army plot so far from home."

"Please, John," I comforted, feeling at the moment only maternal towards him, "you mustn't do this to yourself. Lucy wouldn't want you to grieve like this over what's past. You've got to go on now, make a new life somehow."

He glanced at me, both sorrow and wonder in his eyes. "Do you think it's possible?"

"It must be, John."

"You are a wonderful person, Tamson, stronger than either Lucy or I."

"You're saying that because you once thought you loved me," I reminded him gently. "I simply want to help in any way I can."

He smiled and put my fingers to his lips.

"I have no right to expect anything from you, Tamson. You have a husband and a home and your own happiness now. I merely wanted to see you again, to explain about that night when Lucy and I—"

I withdrew my hand from his. "I want no explanations, John. I understand how you and Lucy felt about each other."

"I don't deserve all this, Tamson." After
a moment he asked quietly, "Are you happy
here?"

I wanted to cry out all the truth to him,
tell him everything that had happened in the
past months, but somehow my pride
wouldn't let me. I had no idea what Breckenridge had written him. As had happened
before, I realized that my stubborn pride was
going to erect a wall around me that would
keep me prisoner. Perhaps that was what
Breckenridge had counted on, why he had
sent for John, knowing that facing him here
at Harlequin, with my legal husband just
outside and the house full of guests, I could
not blurt out my true feelings and just run off
with John Markham—even if he asked me.

John was looking at me curiously, and I
realized he had always been able to understand me better than others. "You aren't
happy, Tamson. Something is the matter. Is
it Breckenridge, or this house—there is an
atmosphere here—tell me what's wrong."

I glanced to him helplessly. I had
needed him, wanted him for so long, and
now he was here. His warmth and sympathy
reached out to me, and suddenly despite all
my resolutions I was in his arms telling him
everything.

When I had finished his face and eyes
were grim. "How could you have let yourself
in for such a thing, Tamson. I—no man is
worth this. My God, the burden I'll carry now
for the rest of my life."

"I don't want to be a burden to you, John," I cried. "I never did; don't you see, that's the whole point?"

He held me gently. "I was a blind, ignorant fool, but I honestly thought you were marrying Breckenridge because you wanted to, because you had found something better. I was so wrapped up in my own affairs, I suppose I willed it to be so. But I would never have allowed you to give yourself to a man like that. You've got to leave here, at once. There can be no more such bargain between you and Rawlins. He must have been mad. Has he been cruel to you? I'll kill him if he has!"

"No," I said quickly. "Not cruel in the sense you mean. It was my own unhappiness more than anything else I think. Please tell me what he wrote to you," I said.

John's eyes were on my hands where he was smoothing my knuckles with his thumbs. "He told me that there had been a bad fire here at Harlequin, that you had not been well, and that he knew it would help cheer you if I came to see you. But he wanted it to be a surprise, a present for you. He told me about the ball, and he enclosed passage money and said he would have his man pick me up the night of the ball. I came, Tamson, not because he asked it, but because I couldn't help myself; I had to see you. I returned his money and came at my own expense. But I suppose I am still his guest, in a way, and so I can't feel free to—say everything I want to say. Why did you feel you had to stay on in such a damnable situation, suffering?"

I gazed up at him through my tears. He took out his handkerchief to wipe my face and answered himself, his voice rough with emotion. "Your cursed pride. Tamson, Tamson, what a mess I've made of both our lives—and Lucy's. I'm not fit to offer my help to any woman, but I've got to get you out of this, back where you belong, where you can start over. You said one had to make a new life—go on, didn't you?"

"Yes," I said, "I believe that if I believe nothing else."

"Then shall I speak to your—husband?"

I straightened my shoulders. "No," I said. "I'll do that. It won't be really difficult. You see, he already knows I'm leaving."

"Yes, but are you sure he will do nothing to stop you?"

"Why should he?" I said. "I agreed to stay till after the ball. I will leave in the morning."

He sat looking at me for a moment and then he said, "Very well, I'll call back for you with a carriage in the morning. We can take the packet north together."

I was smiling, and there was such joy in my heart that I thought it would burst. It would not be the same as it had once been, of course, there would always be the shadows of Lucy and Breckenridge, even of Harlequin House between us, but I felt confident now that in a decent interval of time, when I was truly free, I would be John Markham's wife. If there was guilt in my joy I was not aware of it at the moment. Then John bent, took my face between his hands, and kissed me.

We were interrupted by the sudden opening of the door. Clive Valerian stood there, his face flushed as from anger or drink. He was carrying a square mahogany box in one hand. He frowned slightly at the sight of John and me sitting there holding hands.

"Where's your husband, Mrs. Rawlins?" he demanded. "Where's Breckenridge?"

"I don't know," I replied. "I saw him go out the front door sometime ago."

"How long ago?"

I had no idea how long I had been in the study with John. He answered for me. "Mrs. Rawlins has been here for over an hour."

"Who're you?"

John was not in uniform, I noted, but he got to his feet and answered calmly and with dignity, "I am Captain John Markham, of the United States Army."

"Bluebelly," sneered Clive Valerian.

I saw John flush but he kept his voice even. "Late of the Grand Army of the Republic. We have only one army now, sir, the Army of the United States. The war is over."

Valerian snorted, but his mind for once seemed to be preoccupied with something more important than the late war.

"Have you any idea which direction your husband took?" he asked me.

"No," I said. "I have not, Mr. Valerian. but perhaps I could send a servant—"

He wheeled away abruptly and as he did so the box he was carrying struck against the door jamb, sprang open, and with a clatter spilled a pair of long, ugly looking pistols to the floor.

"What—are you doing with those?" I asked breathlessly.

He had stopped to retrieve them, but he glanced up at me, a malevolent grin on his face and said, "I've every intention of making use of them, ma'am, against your husband." He straightened up, made me a slight bow, and left, slamming the door behind him.

"Who is he?" asked John, puzzled.

"A—neighbor. I'm afraid he and Breckenridge are not on very friendly terms." Then I told him the story, and he listened with deep absorption.

"I had heard rumors of that old duel," he said.

"Do you think he means to harm Breckenridge?"

John frowned. "I don't know. He seems merely to have taken too much to drink."

"It's entirely my fault that he's here tonight," I said. "If something should happen—Oh, John, do you think he would do something dreadful while he is a guest here, even in that condition? I'm sure he can't know what he's doing."

"He looks like a man with a bad temper. If there's bad blood, as you say, it could be preying on his mind—perhaps I'd better go and see if I can find Breckenridge, shall I?" He had gotten to his feet.

"But I'm afraid for you, too, John! Clive Valerian is a violent man. He not only hates Breckenridge, but all Yankees."

John pressed my hand and smiled reassuringly. "Don't worry on my account, Tamson. He's not the first Johnny Reb I've tangled with. Go back to the ballroom."

"No!" I cried, "I want to go with you."

He smiled gently. "It's not the place for you. Stay here then, my dear, if you don't want to return to the others. I'll go and find Breckenridge. You and I can talk again later."

At the door he paused for a moment and said, "Bless you, Tamson, for never changing. I have so much to say to you—but later. Wait for me."

I wanted to cry out that I would wait for him forever, that I had really never stopped waiting for him, but he was gone before I could put my thoughts into words.

Sitting there alone, the music from the ballroom came to my ears in all its warmth and gaiety, yet although I knew I should, I could not force myself to return there. I had to know what was happening.

I went out into the empty hall, but even

the two servants who should have been standing by the door had disappeared. I was just as well pleased, for I wanted no one to see me. I ran lightly up the stairs to my room. I took a dark silk cloak from the closet and flung it over my light ball gown, so that it would not be so conspicuous out of doors. I was back in the main hall when I noted that the door to my husband's suite, next to mine, was open, and I could hear men's voices raised in argument.

I went to the door and knocked briefly. "Breckenridge?"

There were three men in the room and they all wheeled at the sound of my voice. Breckenridge stood the farthest away, by a leather topped desk in the corner, his face partly in shadow. In front of him, their hands still extended as if in argument, stood Virgil Jessup and Pierre Legors.

"What do you want, Tamson?" Breckenridge's voice sounded as remote as an ice flow.

"I—may I see you for a moment, alone?"

"Later," he said curtly. "Have you been out? You had better return to our guests; they will be leaving soon." There was a sudden lashing quality in his tone, as he added. "Or has the most important one left already? I suppose you have just been saying your tender farwells."

I was so angry I could have choked him. I started to turn away in humiliation and fury, and then I remembered why I had been seeking him. No matter how I felt, I owed him at least a warning; with an effort I turned back.

"It's important that I talk to you now." I said steadily, keeping all emotion out of my voice.

"I'm sorry," he replied. "It will have to be later. These gentlemen and I have something to attend to that cannot wait."

Suddenly Virgil Jessup let out an oath. "Breckenridge, I'll be damned if I stand by and let you keep Mrs. Rawlins in ignorance about this!"

"Shut up!" said my husband furiously. "Leave us, Tamson."

"No," said Jessup straightening up his big frame, "you'd better stay a minute, ma'am."

"The truth is," said little Legros sharply, "your husband, madame, has been challenged to a duel by Monsieur Valerian. It is madness, but they will not listen to reason."

"Damn you, Legros!" shouted Breckenridge. "Get out—both of you!"

I stepped into the room as the two men went out, closing the door after them. I had never been in these apartments before, except for the brief moment when I had seen Breckenridge after he had been burned in the fire. They seemed an exact duplicate of my own rooms except that the decor and furnishings were more masculine.

Breckenridge still stood by the desk,

one hand resting lightly on the leather top. "Well," he said impatiently, "what have you to say to me that's so important?"

"About the duel—"

"That has nothing to do with you; it is entirely my affair."

"But that's why I came, to warn you that Clive Valerian was looking for you and that he was armed."

"You knew about it?"

I shook my head. "Not that he had actually challenged you, but that he seemed angry and he had the pistols in a box, and he'd been drinking. He came bursting into the study—"

"And broke up your little *tête-à-tête* with Captain Markham? My deepest sympathies. But you are free to leave now. You have warned me and shown wifely concern in front of my friends."

"Will you stop it!" I shouted. "John is outside somewhere now trying to find you before Clive Valerian does—to stop this ridiculous folly!"

He gave me a thin sardonic grin. "Folly it may be, but if you and Captain Markham had any sense, you would welcome it and let matters take their course. There's a chance the length of time you would have to wait would be much shorter."

"You are a cold-blooded monster, Breckenridge Rawlins! I don't know why I took the trouble to warn you!"

"I don't either. Why did you?"

"Because it was my duty, because it was what any decent person would have done!" I was so angry I could feel the tears stinging my eyelids. "Besides, it's so utterly foolish. Mr. Valerian has been drinking, he doesn't know what he is doing."

"You think I'm going to take advantage of him?"

I ignored that. "Also, there are others to consider, and to continue this feud, this same old business—"

His face hardened. "This is quite another matter, I assure you, and I did not challenge Clive—he challenged me. He has a right to expect satisfaction. If you're worried about him, he isn't half as drunk as he seems; the Valerians never are, and I assure you he could always shoot better drunk than sober."

"But why must you settle anything in this barbaric way?"

"Dueling, my dear, has an old and honored tradition behind it. Since the beginning of time gentlemen have settled their differences by personal combat."

"But what can be so terrible between you that you must end it like this?"

Breckenridge's face had become like a mask. "Valerian set the fire that nearly destroyed Harlequin."

I sank down on the nearest chair. "But—that can't be true!"

"I have the proof—over there." He indicated a pile of soiled and blackened blankets lying on the floor in a corner. "Forbes found them buried under a pile of debris behind the stables tonight, at the exact place where the blaze started. They've been soaked in oil!"

"But anyone could soak blankets in oil!"

He went to get the fragment of one and brought it over to me. It was badly charred but the distinctive white monogram of Marchmount was plainly visible.

"But someone else could have stolen them, put them there to make Clive seem guilty."

"Who would want to?"

I couldn't answer that. "But what reason could he have for doing it?"

"Because of the horses, I suppose. The fire started there at the stable area. He hated the thought of my bringing Harlequin and the stable bloodlines back to their former glory, while Marchmount moldered into ruins. He did it to ruin me, because he despises me, and to destroy Harlequin completely if possible."

"But—he rescued the horses."

"Because he never meant to destroy the horses themselves; he wanted them, and he'd have found some way to get them, buying them up cheaply or something after everything else here was gone."

"It doesn't make sense. He and Seton rescued you, brought you here to the house. They were both burned doing it."

He laughed harshly, the planes of his face stark as he stood above me. "It was his ill luck that someone saw me and gave the alarm, so he had to jump in then and give a show of rescuing me to save his own face later—if I lived. It was his misfortune that I did. It would have been better all around if I had died in that fire."

"Don't say such things! But surely a law court is the place to settle this matter?"

"That's what Virgil and Pierre were trying to persuade me, when you came in."

"They were right; surely you can see that?"

He went to toss the charred blanket in the corner and returned to the desk. I saw him open a drawer and lift out a pair of pearl handled pistols and put them down on the leather top.

"I told you long ago," he said. "You don't know how people feel here in the South. Our personal honor is about all we've got left. It's all Clive Valerian has left, at least. There may be hatred between us, or misunderstanding or whatever you want to call it, but we both come from the same backgrounds, we both still have respect for the names we bear and the traditions they built up and served."

"Tradition!" I scoffed, leaping to my feet and crossing the room towards him. "Is murder more holy done under the guise of tradition?"

He picked up one of the pistols and

examined the hammer, easing it back with his thumb. "These were my great-grandfather's," he said. "They've been used many times, but only justly and in defense of honor."

"No matter what the cause, how can you defend the cold-blooded killing of a man as honorable!"

He put the pistol down and faced me. He seemed like a total stanger, and his chilling aloofness frightened me far more than had any of his rages, or his attempts to make love to me in the Harlequin Room. I did not understand this man who stood before me, but I realized dimly that he was the distillation of the men who for hundreds of years had lived in Harlequin House and defended it with their lives, from without as well as within. It was their ghosts I saw looking out of his dark eyes, their implacable resolve I saw tightening his jawline, their purpose I saw in the curled fingers of his strong hands. I remembered the tale of his ancestor who had killed his bride's lover on her wedding night in my dressing room. I knew then that nothing I could say now would sway him from his decision. I felt a slow despair and hopelessness.

He said quietly, "I think you'd better go, Tamson. This does not concern you in any way. If I have been harsh with you—unkind, tonight or in the past, you must forgive me. Believe me, I had no desire to hurt you. I— hope you will be happy with Markham.

That's why I sent for him. I didn't know then that this was going to happen, but it's better that he is here now."

I stood there thinking of all the things that still remained unsaid, unanswered between us. I wanted to know the truth about Rina; he could afford to be honest with me now. I wanted to tell him I found the secret passage and what I had overheard there, but somehow I couldn't. This was an aloof Rawlins of Harlequin House, not the man I had married and known briefly as my husband. I had done all I could.

"Please go," he said, and there was a trace of weariness in his tone.

"But when do you—"

"In an hour," he said, reading my thoughts. "Down by the river. I want you to be gone by then. Tell Markham to take you in the carriage. You can send for your things later."

"Breckenridge—"

"Go, I tell you!"

I left the room without looking back, feeling as if I had been the betrayer instead of the betrayed.

17

I went out into the hall blindly and stood for a moment with my back to the closed door. Failure is always a bitter thing to face, and yet in all fairness I had done everything in my power to stop this dreadful thing. Where else could I turn? And then I saw Persis standing in the shadows weeping into her handkerchief.

"Persis! Where is Seton?"

Her eyes looked drowned when she raised them to mine. "Oh, Cousin Tamson, what are we to do? Seton's gone to the river bank to be Clive's second!"

"But surely Seton can't condone this senseless duel!"

"He doesn't! But someone came and told him what had happened, and then he found Clive wandering around looking for Breckenridge with those awful pistols under his arm. Seton got the whole story out of him about the blankets, but Clive won't hear of clearing the charges at a trial. He took Seton with him to the river, and sent Virgil Jessup to tell Breckenridge he would expect him at the river in an hour."

"Does everyone know of this, Persis? Aunt Samantha—"

"No," she said quickly, "no one knows. Seton and I were in the garden when the man came to tell us, and then in a little while Clive appeared and took Seton off with him. What are we to do?"

"Surely, Mr. Jessup or Mr. Legros can help?"

"They've tried," said Persis hopelessly.

I knew this was true but was just trying to reassure her.

"Couldn't you do anything with Breckenridge?" she asked.

I shook my head. "He won't listen. He's determined to go through with this thing. He's convinced Clive set fire to Harlequin."

"But if we could prove that he didn't?"

I grabbed her arm. "Can you prove that?"

"No. But I've heard the whole story from Seton and Clive and Mr. Jessup. Maybe Forbes made a mistake? Couldn't we go and talk to him?"

"Yes," I cried instantly. "Come on!"

We met no one on the stairs or in the hall, and we went out onto the veranda facing the front drive. All about us the night throbbed with faint sounds, a breeze had sprung up coming from the river, and the shrubs and leaves of the trees moved in a sprightly dance of their own. Fireflies jigged in and out of the branches like fairy lanterns, cicadas clicked, and the birds and the feet of small animals stirred the leaves and grass on the ground. We could smell the odor of jasmine on the trellis at the end of the house mingled with the still remaining pungent smell of the charred fields. The moon had come up as Honore had promised, a great pale citron globe in the midnight blue sky, accompanied by the flashing brilliance of the stars.

The drive was filled with carriages and horses, the latter coughing and stamping as they flicked away insects with their tails. I saw that most of the drivers stood in a small cluster a little distance away, talking.

I approached them and was relieved to find Jason among them, evidently playing host. He came towards me at once and asked, "Can I help you, Miz Rawlins?"

"Yes," I replied. "Have you seen Forbes?"

It seemed to me that he hesitated longer than necessary before replying, but perhaps I thought it was my overwrought imagination.

"No, ma'am, not since sometime back when he spoke with the master out by the stables, near his cottage."

I thanked him and then with Persis started to walk in that direction.

Jason ran after us. "I'll go git a lantern, ma'am, an' light your way."

"Very well," I said, realizing that since the fire there might be some hazards we would fail to see.

Jason brought the lantern, a very dim one, and we proceeded. As we approached the small log house where the overseer lived, I thought I caught a faint murmur of voices which, while they sounded familiar, I couldn't identify, and I ordered Jason to put out the light.

"Miz Rawlins," he protested, "we need the light!"

"No!" I whispered. "You stay here with Miss Persis, and both of you keep very quiet."

"Yes'm."

Persis clutched my arm for a moment but said nothing.

I went forward on tiptoe. Only a candle seemed to be giving a dull glow through the window of the cottage when I reached it. The coarse cotton curtains had been drawn and the solid door was tightly closed, but due to the hot night the windows were open. Carefully, I moved towards the lighted window and parted the curtains a fraction.

Just as in the Harlequin Room that night, all I could make out were the shadows of two people facing away from me, a man and a woman. But I caught the sheen of fair hair as the woman moved her head, and when she spoke in a low intense tone, I knew who she was.

Rina Vinton!

Even in my amazement at finding her in Forbes' cabin, my brain clearly recorded her speech.

"I tell you we must leave here tonight as we planned. Everything has been attended to, so let it finish itself. Harlequin will be in our hands now, and when the time comes no court of law will be able to dispute that."

Forbes laughed in a disagreeable way. "You're pretty keen, Rina, finding out he wanted to repay his wife for the money she loaned him for Harlequin when they married."

"It was my womanly sympathy, Sam dear. He couldn't help but lay all his troubles at my feet—like he used to do with Ana-belle." A hardness had come into her voice. "The note he signed for the money I advanced him to repay Tamson is something he will never be able to make good now. It was worth selling Bellehaven to get the money. We can afford to go away for a while, and when the time is ripe, we will return to claim Harlequin House." She laughed harshly. "And now Clive Valerian will finish the master of Harlequin. We had only to fan the flames of their old hatred, and of course Tamson played into our hands by inviting Clive here. What did Breckenridge say when you showed him the burned saddle-blankets tonight?"

"He was right furious."

"He believed you? There was no suspicion that you had stolen the blankets and used them?"

"He believed what he saw; how could he help it? After all, I've been a trusted employee of Harlequin, haven't I?"

Rina laughed again. "I sent a note to Clive telling him what Breckenridge had found, and that he was coming to accuse him. I watched him go and get the box of dueling pistols he always carries in his carriage. No one will be able to dispute that it wasn't a fair fight between two gentlemen defending their honor. And if either of them lives, he will be shunned because of what people know of their past. How I've planned and waited for this moment! At last my poor sister Anabelle will be avenged on the two stiff-necked men who let her go to her death rather than marry her! They'll pay for that now. Neither of them will be able to forget this night if they live! It's right that they should destroy each other, and that Harlequin should go down with them. How I've hated this ancient aristocratic pile with all its bloody secrets that was considered too good for my sister!"

"Her child," mused Forbes, "was it Valerian's?"

"No, some wretch of a sailor she met in Charleston, but Valerian had proposed, and when he found out about the other man he went back on his word, though he kept her secret. Breckenridge, the fool, believed her an innocent wronged by Clive Valerian, but he made no move to marry her, and in a panic she killed herself. She should have been mistress of Harlequin, not that snow-maiden northerner with all her miser's gold!''

I flushed with hot anger, yet so much of what had happened was growing clear now. They had used the passage to frighten me, wanting me away from Harlequin as soon as possible, once I had been made use of to get Breckenridge into a hole he could not climb out of. I heard Rina's voice going on in triumph, ''She'll want no part of Harlequin now. She's afraid, and I convinced Breckenridge to send for John Markham. Breckenridge had completely forgotten giving Anabelle a key to the Harlequin Room, where they used to meet. It was all so easy to frighten her!''

I clenched my hands at my sides. Somehow these two evil, greedy schemers had succeeded in fooling all of us. They had spread fear and deceit at every turn, and like hungry fish we had swallowed the tainted bait. While I stood silently, undecided what to do, I saw two hands come around Rina's back—two bandaged hands! I had forgotten Forbes had been burned in the fire, too! They were *his* hands I had seen that night in the Harlequin Room, not Breckenridge's! It had been Sam Forbes embracing Rina, as he was now. Breckenridge had meant everything he had ever said to me; there had never been anyone else in his mind or his heart. My thoughts were in a turmoil, but there wasn't time now to stop and sort them out. Somewhere along the river bank in the night, death stalked Breckenridge and Clive Valerian, all because of these two evil people embracing in front of me. I wanted to face them with the wreckage of their plans, but there wasn't time for that either.

I whirled from the window and beckoned to Jason. "Get some men quickly and quietly, and surround this cabin," I whispered sternly. "On pain of death you are not to allow either Forbes or Miss Rina to leave here until I return, do you understand?"

He looked confused but nodded his head.

As a further clincher I added, "There is a plot afoot to murder the master."

"Yes, ma'am! I do what you say!" He scurried off, and I went to whisper as much as I had time for into Persis' ear, instructing her to go back to the house for some of the men to come and help us. Then when I stilled her shocked exclamations, I demanded to know the way to the river dueling grounds.

"Wait till some of the men can go with you," she pleaded.

"No, I must go at once. Tell me."

"It's not far—you go on behind the stableyard, along the fence and over the little bridge. There's a wide grassy place along the bank on the right. That's it."

I lit the lantern Jason had left, seeing him already returning with a group of armed men, and made my way as quickly as possible to the fence in the rear. I followed it to the path that led to the short wooden bridge. Moonlight shone full on the river now, making it shimmer like crushed foil, and to my right, a little lower down near the bank, I could make out several figures standing on the thick grassy sward. I caught the sound of anger in their voices and my heart gave a leap as I heard John cry out:

"You can't do this thing! There's no clear proof either way! I beg you wait and let the courts decide."

I could see Breckenridge and Clive Valerian in their shirtsleeves, each holding a long ugly pistol in his hand, arms at their sides. They stood some paces apart facing each other with the seconds nearby, while John stood between them turning first to one then the other, his hands thrust out in entreaty.

"You want proof?" cried Breckenridge. "Go look at the charred blankets in my bedroom! Forbes found them tonight just where the fire started. Five blankets, each with the Marchmount name on them. Valerian set out deliberately to ruin Harlequin and me!"

I heard Clive Valerian swear. "You damned blind fool!" He stepped a few paces closer in his anger.

"You don't know those blankets weren't stolen from Marchmount, and used by someone else to throw suspicion on Valerian," argued John reasonably. "Wait until you have better proof of his guilt than this, Breckenridge."

"I can believe Forbes—and my own eyes," said Breckenridge bitterly.

"No, no, you can't!" I cried out. "He lied—it isn't true!"

But my words were drowned out by Clive Valerian's roar, "You damned idiot, Rawlins, let's end this thing the only way it can ever be ended. Get out of the way, Markham, this has nothin' to do with you, bluebelly!"

Suddenly he straightened and stepped forward. He raised his arm and in one motion brought it down on John's head savagely. I saw John fall like a chopped tree and I cried out, but neither Clive nor Breckenridge glanced in my direction.

In horror, I saw each of them raise their pistols and take deadly and deliberate aim.

Although I know I shrieked out a string of words, they were completely unintelligible to me and must have seemed so to the others grouped there. In some far recess of my mind I dimly heard the report of shots, I saw Clive Valerian flinch, and watched Breckenridge standing straight and completely motionless, until he suddenly pitched forward on his face and lay absolutely still.

In that horrifying moment when I realized that everything linking us was over, when I knew it was no use, I understood with a terrible clarity that I loved him—that I must always have loved him.

18

Oddly, at that most devastating moment of my life, I didn't faint. I stood for a second, stunned and motionless, then picked up my skirts and started to run.

I remember I had reached Breckenridge before the others and somehow managed to turn him over, and was sitting in the damp grass pillowing his head in my lap when Clive Valerian came up.

Dully, I saw that his left sleeve was wet with blood, and that he still carried a pistol in his right hand. Suddenly, with a look of revulsion, he threw the pistol from him into the river.

I realized that John had come to kneel beside me, and there was a livid bruise on his temple. One of the other men, Mr. Jessup, I think, opened Breckenridge's white shirt and bared his chest, now covered with blood. He lay with his eyes closed, a lock of dark hair falling over his forehead, looking strangely peaceful and more youthful than I could remember seeing him before.

I glanced up at Clive Valerian, tears blurring my sight and cried, "You're a murderer!" Then brokenly, in near hysteria, I told them what I had overheard in Forbes' cabin.

I saw Clive's face go deadly white, but he spoke to John and to Virgil Jessup, not to me, saying roughly. "Is he—dead?"

Seton had been pressing his handkerchief to the ugly chest wound. I clutched Breckenridge closer to me, my tears falling on his pale cheeks.

"The wound's still bleeding," he said tersely, "we've got to get him back to the house." He glanced at me compassionately, and seeming to think action the best remedy to my shock, added, "Run ahead, Tamson, and warn them we're coming and that your husband is badly hurt. Is there a doctor at the ball?" he asked his brother.

"Yes, Dr. Malcolm from Croix."

"Go with Tamson then and tell him we'll need his services, and he'd better start with you. See that Clive has a stiff brandy, Tamson. We'll be there as quickly as possible. And don't worry about Forbes," he added grimly, "these other gentlemen and I will take care of him."

Clive nodded and Mr. Jessup helped me to my feet. I left reluctantly, but fear for my husband and a very small, dull hope, lent wings to my feet.

Everything that happened after we left the river bank was shrouded in a merciful blur of haste. I saw the doctor and some of the men carry Breckenridge to his room, and Honore joined them there. They would not let me go inside, and so I sat in a chair in the hall, dimly aware of people leaving the house and then of the great silence that followed.

Aunt Samantha for once was quiet and capable, and Persis and Seton never left my side. John came and went from the chair where I sat, consulting with the doctor and Honore at intervals, and giving me what comfort he could. Once he bent down, and holding my hand, whispered in my ear. "You love him very much, don't you? I saw it in your face there at the river."

And though I could only nod through my tears, he pressed my fingers and said, "Now you know what it's like, Tamson. Even—if you lose, as I did, you will never be alone again."

But my heart sank inside me at his words, as the thought tore through me: Breckenridge doesn't know! If he dies he'll never know that I love him!

I prayed as I watched the bedroom door throughout the long night, my eyes dull now and red-rimmed, but none of them could make me relinquish my place in the hall.

As the first dawn was breaking and I heard the now familiar magical trill of a mockingbird, Honore and John came from the bedroom looking weary and subdued. Honore gave me a searching and enigmatic glance, then moved off down the hall without speaking.

My heart seemed to stop beating as John came to squat down by my chair, taking both my hands in his.

"Tamson—"

"John, tell me quickly. I can't stand anymore."

"The doctor removed the ball. He thinks that with care, Breckenridge has a good chance to recover."

I burst into tears of relief and gratitude, covering my face with my hands.

It was that night, after a long and dreamless sleep, that I heard that both Rina and Forbes were now in jail at Croix, charged with arson, fraud and attempted murder.

It was many days after that before the doctor pronounced Breckenridge out of danger, and I was permitted at last to visit him.

I entered his bedroom almost shyly, but I need not have felt that way. He lay pale and drawn looking, but he smiled and held out his hand to me. I took it and felt him draw me closer to the bed.

"Breckenridge, I—"

He stopped me before I could go on. "They've told me everything, Tamson. I've indeed been the fool Clive Valerian accused me of being. It seems we were all pawns in a very dirty game. I owe Clive an apology, and I owe you—even more. John Markham is a fine man. At least I gave you one gift I knew you would like. You belong together."

I stared at him in disbelief. He still didn't know how I felt about him! Then I realized that John had gallantly left the privilege of telling him to me. But I was suddenly lost and confused; I couldn't just blurt it out like a schoolgirl, not after all that had been between us. How could I convince him that it was true? Yet I knew that I had to say something, he was looking at me so steadily.

"John is one of the finest men alive," I began softly, "but I'm afraid *he* is something of a fraud. He's let you go on thinking that we intend to marry someday?"

Breckenridge frowned. "But that's the only way it could end. I sent for him, knowing how much you longed to be with him. I— couldn't help reading the postscript to your letter to Mrs. Campbell that day." He looked suddenly embarrassed.

"Just as I couldn't help thinking it was you there in the Harlequin Room making love to Rina, that night I discovered the secret passage, I saw what I thought were your bandaged hands; I didn't know that Forbes had burned his hands too, and that they were bandaged like yours, until I saw him that night in his cabin with Rina."

"He started the fire," said Breckenridge, "planning to put the blame on Clive. He claimed of course that he had been trying to put out the fire."

"I know that now," I said. "As for John, he was always really in love with Lucy, and he always will be. I've discovered that true love is like that; it doesn't change."

He glanced away from me, a trace of the old bitterness on his mouth. "I—know."

"But what you don't know," I said quietly, feeling my heart begin to beat heavily inside my breast, "is that sometimes you can fight so hard against it, that you don't know it's real love at all. Just as I fought against my feeling for—you."

He turned swiftly to stare at me, then a slow wonder broke over his tired face.

I glanced down at my hands and went on breathlessly. "I love you, Breckenridge. I must have loved you all along, only you treated me so lordly and cold at first, that I couldn't admit my feelings even to myself. I thought I loved John, and I will always be very fond of him, but I realize now that I might never have known what real love was if you hadn't come along and bullied me into marrying you."

When I looked up he was smiling broadly at me. "It seemed the only way to get you at the time. It was worth whatever it cost," he said softly.

I felt his hands reach out and draw me down towards him.

"But I promise," he added solemnly, "never to gamble with your love again."

"Nor," I said, "with your own life, or Harlequin. Promise?"

But after he kissed me all he said, and all that mattered was, "I love you, Tamson Rawlins."